BRENDA
OF BEECH HOUSE

by
DOROTHEA MOORE

COLLINS CLEAR-TYPE PRESS
LONDON AND GLASGOW

THIS BOOK IS DEDICATED
WITH MY LOVE
TO
BETTY WILSON

CONTENTS

CONTENTS

BRENDA OF BEECH HOUSE

CHAPTER I

SIR REGINALD'S SOLUTION

BRENDA had finished her prep and put it away tidily in the deep drawer of her writing-table, in readiness for her different instructors next morning. Then she went and stood by the big window looking on the square of garden, which was the especial property of her younger brother Carol and herself.

The laughing April daylight still lingered about it, and daffodils of every known variety made a brave show. Brenda half thought she would go out, and pick a bunch for the table in her father's special sitting-room; he had been quite pleased when she and Carol took him in a handful of the first daffodils from the south border. But then there would be all the fuss of ringing for her maid to go with her, as Miss Heron was

off duty; and Annette always found it too
cold, or the grass too damp, or something
silly, unless it happened to be exactly the
usual time for going out. Brenda came to
the conclusion that she wasn't keen enough
to make it worth while; besides, she might
miss Carol if she went into the garden, and
she particularly wanted to catch him directly
he came in, to tell him that Miss Heron
was out, and he and she might do something
really exciting, like toasting cheese for supper.
Brenda opened the window as wide as it
would go, and leant out at an angle which
would certainly have been stopped at once
by Miss Heron as dangerous. But she felt
that she wanted to get as far away as possible
from the dull old schoolroom, where so much
of her time was unwillingly passed.

The soft spring breeze ruffled her long
hair, stirring up a grievance. Her request
to be bobbed or shingled had been turned
down most uncompromisingly by her father,
and she had to endure long thick hair, which
refused to keep tidy, and got her into trouble
often by the refusal, and was brushed night
and morning for ten minutes by a perfect
maid who knew her duty and made Brenda's
head absolutely tingle. "Carol always has
the luck," she muttered rebelliously, pushing

back the hair that blew into her eyes;
" it's pretty unfair to me."

Somehow the beauty of the spring garden
into which she was looking gave no pleasure
to Brenda this evening. The high walls
which surrounded it, and made it so sheltered
and sunny a place, seemed to her, just now,
so typical of her own life.

" I shall be fourteen in June," she thought
to herself, " and except for a few stupid
processions and things I've never seen or
done anything, except stick in these dull
rooms, and these silly gardens and park. I
shouldn't mind if I were going to Eton as
Carol is next year, or if Father would let
me do things as he does Carol. But it's
nothing but lessons and governesses and dull
walks and rides all by myself from morning
till night. Oh, I'm sick of it ! "

Brenda thought she heard footsteps in the
passage, and drew her head in hastily. But
it was a false alarm ; no Carol yet. She
walked restlessly across to the big, old-
fashioned bookcase, with glass doors, behind
which lived the carefully selected story-books
she was allowed to read. Mainly historical
and classics. School stories were most
decidedly discouraged in her schoolroom.
And somehow it was a school story which

Brenda seemed to want just then. She
stood looking at the titles, and wondering
which book she knew least well; took out
a couple, glanced at them, and decided that
she didn't want to read. She seemed to
know all her own books by heart, and Carol's
books lived in his study, and though he was
always willing enough to lend, no book might
be brought into the schoolroom without
reference to Miss Heron.

On the upper shelves of the handsome
bookcase were such children's books as
Brenda's English mother had brought from
her English home—*Little Women*—some of
Miss Yonge's historical stories, and again,
above those, books by which Brenda's grand-
mother, her father's mother, had been intro-
duced to the English language in her youth
—*Parents' Assistant*, *Rasselas*, and Scott's
Poems. Brenda did not feel just then as
though she wanted to read any one of them all.

She wandered slowly round the schoolroom in search of some better amusement.
It was a fine, handsome room, but little
furniture had been changed since the grand-
father and great-aunts of Brenda and Carol
unwillingly struggled along the path of learning there. Every single article of furniture
was large, handsome, solid, and dull.

Brenda was thinking so, discontentedly, for about the hundredth time, when she caught at last the sound for which she had been waiting—her brother Carol's footsteps in the corridor. She rushed across the room and opened the door.

" There you are at last—you *are* late ! "

Carol hurried in. He was a fair-haired, delicate-looking boy, small for nearly twelve years, and not nearly so good-looking as his sister. He wore a miniature uniform of the 1st Mont Chasseurs—so called from the days when the crack corps had to fight for the King's supremacy with rebellious mountaineers—dark green, with the eagle's feather, once worn in the hat, now worked on the left breast, with the motto of the corps, " To have—to hold."

Brenda put her arm round her brother's shoulders and drew him to the window. " Come in and sit down and tell me about it. Did you open it all right, and did you feel nervous, and were the speeches frightfully long, and what made you so late ? And won't you be thankful to get away from reviews and opening museums and hospitals and giving away prizes, and go to an English school—you lucky boy ! "

Carol glanced rather nervously at the

clock. " I can't stay more than five
minutes, Brenda. I've got to change——"

" You needn't—Miss Heron's away, thanks
be. Shall we tell them to bring us cheese
and we'll toast it and . . ."

Carol looked worried. " I shan't be able
to, I'm afraid. Father has sent to say I'm
to dine to-night to meet somebody."

" Carol—you've not ! "

" I'm awfully sorry," apologised Carol.
He knew of old what a sore point it was with
the sister nearly two years his senior that
their father believed so uncompromisingly in
a retired schoolroom life for his daughter,
while expecting the Crown Prince, though
under equally strict rule, to take some part
in public functions. And of late, to add to
this ever-rankling grievance, there had been
something even worse to bear.

Carol, whose mother had died at his birth,
had never been strong, and his doctor had
strongly advised for him at least a year at
a seaside preparatory school, before he went
to Eton. Brenda had known for the last
three months that Carol was going to
Rollincourt, a preparatory school at Rotherbay, next term, and she was to be left to
endure the dull schoolroom at the Palace
all alone. Her petitions to be sent to

England to school as well had been vetoed by King Conrad, her father, and Brenda was feeling rather at odds with life just now.

Carol's defection was somehow the last straw. " It isn't fair," she cried passionately. " Oh, don't be silly, Carol ; of course it isn't your fault ; I'm not angry with you. But why should I always have to be second fiddle, because you happen to be Crown Prince ? I shall go and ask Father if I mayn't dine to-night as well as you."

" Brenda ! Don't ! " urged Carol, catching at her sleeve. " Father will be vexed. I'm awfully sorry about dining—I wouldn't if I could help it, you know. I would much rather do the toasting cheese up here. It is hard lines on you—but don't, don't go down till you're sent for."

Brenda wasn't particularly patient at any time, and now she was too much exasperated to think of prudence. " Well, I can't help it if Father is annoyed. He should give me a chance," she flared, and pulled herself from Carol's hold, and made a bolt for her bedroom. Even her daring shrank at the idea of presenting herself before her father with ink down her nails. A hasty scurry, an angry bang or so to her hair with the brush, and she was flying down the corridors

towards the grand staircase, heedless of
Carol's rather nervous offer, " Shall I ask
for you ? "

At the door of the King's library she was
stopped, as she expected, by the officer of
the guard before she had time to knock.

" Pardon me, Princess, but His Majesty
is giving informal audience to the English
Minister."

" Please ask my father to receive me at
once ; it's very important," Brenda urged.

The young officer considered. " A little
later, Princess . . ."

Brenda sprang past him and knocked
loudly on the door. The King's voice,
raised rather irritably, called, " Come in ! "

Brenda opened the door, with its heavy
curtain, and came in. Then she curtsied
and stood still, waiting for permission to
advance.

Her father was sitting back in a great
arm-chair ; the English Minister, rather a
friend of hers and Carol's, sat opposite.
Both were smoking. It was evidently a
quite informal interview.

But King Conrad did not seem to approve
of the interruption, for all its informality.
" You, Brenda ? What are you doing
here ? " he asked, with cold displeasure,

while the Minister stood up and bowed,
before taking the hand which Brenda held
out.

"Father, I wanted so much to see you . . ."

"Surely you are old enough to know that
you should wait until I send for you," said
the King.

"Yes, sir, I know, and it wasn't Captain
Saradin's fault, so please don't be vexed
with him. He told me you were receiving,
and he didn't let me in. But I simply had
to come and ask you something."

"You may sit down," said her father.

Brenda sat down, feeling her legs rather
shaky quite suddenly.

"Would Your Majesty perhaps give me
permission to withdraw?" suggested the
Minister.

"No. Pray remain, Sir Reginald," said
the King.

He looked Brenda over with his grey eyes
which could seem as cold and as hard as
ice. "You may inform me—briefly—what
is the urgent business which prevented you
from recollecting the claims of good
manners," he said, and Brenda wished Sir
Reginald Rownham considerably farther.
But she had plenty of courage of her own,
and since her father was undeniably very

angry, she saw no harm in making him rather angrier, in the principle of being as well hanged for a sheep as a lamb.

"I'm nearly two years older than Carol, but it's he who sits up and does everything," she said. "Mayn't I sit up as well, to-night, Father? It is so dreadfully dull in the schoolroom all by myself, and it will be worse than ever when Carol has gone to school. Mayn't I just dine to-night, Father?"

"No, Brenda," the King said inexorably.

Brenda choked with anger; then she found her voice.

"Then won't you reconsider about school for me?" she said in a low voice. "You can't want me here, because you hardly ever have me with you . . ."

"That will do, Brenda; you have my permission to retire," her father interrupted, and Brenda stood up and curtsied mechanically. There seemed nothing else to do. As the Minister was closing the door behind her, she heard her father, who had watched her out in a cold silence, ask a question of Sir Reginald: "You have experience in daughters, Sir Reginald?" and Sir Reginald's half-laughing answer: "Well, sir, mine go to school."

CHAPTER II

ONE WAY OF DOING IT

THE Easter holidays had begun, and Brenda and Carol were spending them at Castle Helsingfoss in the Forest. For a blissful fortnight strict discipline was to be relaxed, and then Carol was to start for his English school, and poor Brenda to go back to a life with no companionship of her own age at all.

Her father had taken no further notice either of her breach of etiquette in interrupting an audience or of her indignant protest in the unfairness of her position. But then the holidays had begun only two days after that unfortunate evening, and she and Carol went to Helsingfoss and only saw their father now and then when he motored over from the capital for a few ill-spared hours.

It was a glorious time, and Brenda was determined to enjoy it to the uttermost, letting no thought of the gloomy future spoil her fun if she could help it.

The weather was perfect as April can be. Except for an occasional scudding shower, it was a fortnight of almost uninterrupted sunshine.

The Forest, which encroached upon the Castle grounds on every side, smelt spicy and delicious, and was full of bursting life; and the boy and girl were out in it from morning till night.

Carol's governor, a kindly old man, once a famous soldier, and Mademoiselle Panache, the governess with Brenda, left their charges to themselves within reasonable limits; and they were quite alone, as it happened, when they tumbled on the picnic party close by the Otter's Pool on a glorious sunny afternoon, when they had been nearly a week at Helsingfoss.

They had not really meant to go so far, but a difference of opinion about a short-cut had landed them three miles at least from the Castle; and it was tea-time.

The picnickers were having tea in a clearing—such an attractive tea, with a gipsy kettle boiling away and all kinds of good things spread out on little cardboard plates with crimped edges.

The picnickers looked such a jolly set, too. There were girls—one about Brenda's own size and one bigger—and two tinies; there were three boys—one very tall and the other two a good deal smaller than he was—and a pleasant-looking middle-aged lady who sat on a camp-stool and looked carefully in her cup, before she drank, for signs of insect life. All were chattering away in English, which Brenda had been taught to speak almost from her cradle, and in which she and Carol talked to each other nearly as often and as easily as in their own language.

And suddenly Brenda knew that she was dying for a drink, for the afternoon was quite extraordinarily hot for the time of the year. She hesitated for a moment; they seemed to have oceans of tea, this picnic party, but Mademoiselle Panache would be so dreadfully shocked at the idea of her princess actually asking for a cup. In that moment that she stood undecided, one of the girls looked across to the other side of the clearing and saw her.

" Hullo ! " she said affably.

After that, of course, Brenda had to speak. She walked into the clearing.

" I hope you didn't think us rude ? " she said in English to the lady on the camp-stool ; " but your picnic looked so jolly."

" Well, as you have stopped, have some

tea, won't you ? " the girl who had spoken
before invited hospitably. " They can, can't
they, Mrs. Reresby ? "

" Certainly, if they like," the lady on the
camp-stool addressed as Mrs. Reresby said,
most pleasantly. " Come and find places
in the circle, both of you. We have a spare
mug, I know, and perhaps you won't mind
sharing ?   You have the sandwiches, M. M."

Brenda sat down thankfully by the girl
who had spoken to her. She was evidently
" M. M.," and looked about her own age.
" Thank you, that will be lovely ; I am so
thirsty."

" It's awfully good of you," murmured
Carol, equally thankful, though more shy
about it. The two wayfarers were promptly
supplied with tea that tasted only a little
of smoke, and everything that they could
possibly want in the food line.

Their hosts were too polite to ask names,
and Brenda refrained from volunteering
them lest the party should happen to know
what the Crown Prince of Nystrea and his
sister happened to be called. The fun,
which was fast and furious at present, might
dry up into stiffness and politeness if M. M.
and the rest of them knew that they were
entertaining royalty.

Mrs. Reresby was the mother of the tall boy and the older girl; and the girl was a House Captain at Beech House, Rotherbay; Brenda got that very soon. It seemed that the big boy had been at Rollincourt, but was now at Rugby; that the two small boys were his cousins and going to Rollincourt next term, and M. M. and the two younger girls were all at Beech House, and the whole party were spending the Easter holidays in Nystrea.

"What's Beech House like?" Brenda asked, deeply interested.

The big boy spread himself luxuriously among the primroses. "I'll tell you. Beech House is a school where none of the girls do any work, as far as I can see, because of the two or three 'delicates' that get shot in among 'em every term; so they have the time of their lives while fellows are swotting, and——"

M. M. and the two small girls rose in wrath.

"You don't know anything about it, Bertram," M. M. indignantly informed him. "Margaret, you tell him, won't you?"

Margaret laughed. "Bertram is only trying to get a rise out of us, M. M. Keep calm!"

Brenda spoke before M. M. could demand satisfaction from the shameless Bertram.

" Do tell me what Beech House is like, really and honestly. I'm awfully keen to know about school."

" Aren't you at school ? " asked M. M. with directness. " I didn't know that anybody wasn't nowadays—of your size, I mean."

" It isn't my fault that I'm not," Brenda said bitterly ; and Carol, listening to her anxiously, chimed in at that point with her request, " Do tell us about Beech House."

M. M. obliged, with some assistance from the small girls, and an occasional correction from Margaret, or ribald interpolation from Bertram. When they had finished, Brenda sighed enviously. " Oh, I do wish I could go there ! "

" Ask your people," suggested Margaret practically.

" I have asked my father, and he won't."

" What a shame ! " M. M. cried. " Can't you tease him till he says yes ? "

" I don't think that would help," observed Carol nervously.

One of the two small girls—Brenda had not decided which answered to the name of Penny and which to Pris — put in her oar at this point. " It seems almost a pity you

can't be a ' delicate ' like Katharine-Ursula,
then you'd get sent."

" Don't you think we ought to be getting
on, Brenda ? " Carol said hastily. " They
will worry at home if we're much later."

Brenda recognised the voice of duty,
though without enthusiasm. " Yes, I suppose we ought," she acknowledged, getting
up. " It's so jolly here one forgets all about
time. Good-bye, Mrs. Reresby, and thank
you ever so much for asking us to tea. We
have so enjoyed it, and meeting you all."

" You worry your father about Beech
House ; and next term is the nicest to start
in," was M. M.'s parting remark. Bertram's
good-bye, like that of all the rest, was
pleasant enough ; unfortunately his comment on the guests was made before Brenda,
for whom Carol was clearing a way through
some rather thick undergrowth, was absolutely out of hearing :

" Yes, nice kids enough ; but the girl
thinks too much of herself, doesn't she ? "

Brenda boiled with indignation. Did
this horrid superior kind of boy dare to hold
her father's view—that the second place was
all that belonged to Princess Brenda ? Her
only comfort was that Carol had not heard.

Brenda was very silent as she and Carol

hurried back, rather in fear of a scolding, through the three miles of forest that lay between the picnic party and Castle Helsingfoss.

Beech House sounded such fun—few rules, heaps of games, interesting lessons in a class where there would be some point in doing well because of the competition; bathing with a crowd of girls instead of alone with a swimming mistress in attendance; Guides —an unknown thrill to Brenda—hosts of friends, and best of all, no longer that galling sense of inferiority at every turn which met her in the home where she must always be a bad second to the Crown Prince.

" Didn't it sound a gorgeous place ? " she said to Carol—" Beech House, I mean."

" Yes," Carol agreed. " I would have liked to ask that boy something about Rollincourt too."

Brenda remembered that she had demanded information exclusively about Beech House, and never thought of Carol. The recollection made her cross.

" Well, you'll know all about it in a week or two, anyway," she said. " There's no need for you to grouse; I think you're uncommonly lucky to be one of the ' delicates,' as that small girl called it."

Directly she had said that, Brenda knew that it had been rather a mean thing to say. Carol hated to be reminded of his delicacy ; he flushed uncomfortably. Brenda would probably have told him that she hadn't meant it, if Mademoiselle Panache had not dashed upon them from a side path at the moment in a great state of discomposure and heat.

" Where have you hidden yourselves ? " she demanded. " We search everywhere— the General and myself, and presently also the servants. His Majesty arrived at tea-time, and behold you were not ! "

" Oh, I am sorry ! Were you frightened, Mademoiselle, and did Father mind ? " Carol asked. " We went too far, and some kind people gave us tea. But how dreadful to have missed Father."

" He is not departed," Mademoiselle Panache informed them, calming a little. " He remains to-night, and desires that you both dine with him."

" Oh, I am to dine this time, am I ? " Brenda asked glumly. She was not particularly pleased, to tell the exact truth, by the news of her father's coming. It meant so much extra washing and brushing and changing, and though when she and Carol had meals alone with their father, conversation was permitted, she usually found it best to consider what she said before she said it. King Conrad could snub in the most annihilating way, and his attitude towards slang, slurred consonants, and opinionated views was cold in the extreme.

She went upstairs with her governess to get ready for dinner with the meticulous care demanded by the occasion, feeling irritated. And she did not get less irritated as the dressing went on. Mademoiselle Panache fussed, and Annette fussed; and her hair had tied itself into witches' knots in the course of scrambling through undergrowth that was also tangled, and earth had got down her nails in the way earth does when you dig up primrose roots without a trowel; and wherever King Conrad of Nystrea might be, dinner was on the table at half-past seven precisely.

Brenda was ready, but only just in time, and shot into the drawing-room to join Carol barely a quarter of a minute before the double doors opened to admit the King.

Her frock was of a delicate pale green, very fresh and cool-looking; but the girl inside it felt nearly red-hot between hurry and fret of spirit. Her father noticed her flushed face as he kissed her.

" You are very hot, Brenda ; are you not well ? "

" It seems almost a pity you can't be a ' delicate ' like Katharine-Ursula, then you'd get sent——"

The remark, in Pris' little clear voice— or was it Penny's ?—flashed across Brenda's mind as the question came, and with it a temptation. " Oh, I'm tired, Father," she said.

" H'm," said the King ; " that sounds more like Carol."

He glanced at her with some attention as the three sat down to the little dinner-table set in the great window of the dining-room that looked upon the Forest.

Brenda caught that look, and her hopes rose suddenly. If her father could only be brought to think that her health needed attention as well as her brother's ! She laid down her spoon, after two spoonfuls of the soup, and refused omelette, though she liked savoury omelette very particularly.

Her father interrupted Carol's account of their holiday adventures to remark : " Why, you're not very hungry for a girl who has been living in the Forest, Brenda."

" We met some awfully kind people pic-
nicking this afternoon who gave us a lot of
their tea," Carol explained ; and Brenda
could have beaten him with pleasure at the
moment.

But her father only said : " Indeed ; who
were they ? " and listened quite kindly while
Carol told him who they were, and the
important fact that one had been to Rollincourt and two were going there ; and the
girls were at a school in the same place.
" They told us quite a lot about it, sir, and it
sounded ever so nice, didn't it, Brenda ? " he
concluded, with an evident desire to bring
his sister more into the conversation.

" Yes," Brenda agreed shortly, without
seconding his attempt. She would have
liked to point out that it wasn't much of a
pleasure to hear about schools when you
were debarred from going to any ; but remarks of that kind did not go down well
with King Conrad. So she just picked
languidly at her roast chicken without adding
anything to the monosyllable.

" What was the name of the girls' school ? "
asked her father. The question might have
been meant for either. Carol answered it :

" It was Beech House, sir."

" Oh," said the King, and watched his

daughter in silence for a moment as she sent away her almost untouched plate.

" And did you acquire any useful information about Rollincourt from the boy who had been there ? " he wanted to know of Carol, after a moment.

" Well, we were talking mostly about Beech House, I think," Carol explained, with an almost apologetic glance towards his sister.

" Which is more, apparently, than Brenda wishes to do now," her father commented. " What, no meringues, Brenda ? I imagine they have been sent in on purpose for you."

" No, thank you, Father," Brenda said steadily, though she gave the silver dish of meringues a distinctly regretful glance.

King Conrad smiled a little, then he said : " I suppose among the many facts told you about Beech House was not included one— that girls are sometimes sent there on account of health ? "

Brenda, whose face had cooled in the coolness of the big bay window, suddenly flamed again.

" In case it is news to you, they are," he went on, rather drily ; " though that does not happen to be precisely the reason for which you are going to Beech House next term."

CHAPTER III

BEECH HOUSE

MISS HERON, who had brought Brenda and Carol to their respective schools, had been gone for exactly one minute. Brenda, standing in the window of the drawing-room at Beech House while Miss Christopherson saw her visitor to the door, was feeling a little—odd. She wasn't nervous—Brenda hardly knew what that feeling was—but the ground was uncommonly new.

And yet the drawing-room, with its dainty low tea-table at which she had just made an excellent tea, was very much like other drawing-rooms where she had been received when she was allowed to go out. The difference accounting for the feeling of oddity was that now she wasn't being " received "; she was just a new girl at Beech House.

Miss Christopherson came back. She was quite middle-aged, but exceedingly good-looking, and though not particularly tall, possessed of more quiet dignity than any one whom Princess Brenda had come across in all her life before.

" Ah, you are having a look at the garden, Brenda ? " she said. " This particular part is my private property, and girls don't come into it without an invitation from me. Presently we will introduce you to the tennis courts and the shrubbery and the lake, as the girls call it, though that is rather too grand a name."

" Thanks, I shall like that," Brenda said politely.

" Had you quite finished tea before Miss Heron went ? You had ? Then sit down, my dear, and we will have a little talk before I introduce you to the other girls."

" I know some of them—your girls, I mean —already," Brenda said, sitting down upon the sofa beside Miss Christopherson— " Margaret Somebody, and M. M."

Miss Christopherson smiled. " Mariota Mountnessing—I think a shortened form is very justified in her case—I am glad you know her. I am putting you in a three-bed room with M. M. and a girl called Katharine Venning. I hope you will all get on very well together, and that you, Brenda, who are, I know, quite new to school, will be particular about remembering rules."

" I spend half my time at home in being told not to do things," Brenda remarked.

" I dare say. But here we don't spend our time in telling girls to keep rules ; we expect them to think and remember. It will all seem a little strange at first, I dare say, but it is sure to be a help that you know M. M. already."

" And Margaret—Reresby, that was the name, I think," said Brenda easily.

" Margaret Reresby is senior House Captain, and a very important person here," Miss Christopherson told her. " I don't suppose you will have much to do with Margaret unless you lose marks to B. House ; and we will hope you don't do that ! I want you to be a happy and successful Beech House girl, Brenda ; and if you find you have a little more to learn than other people do, don't be discouraged. By your father's wish no difference will be made between you and the other girls—and that will make everything very much easier for you, you will find. And now we will send for M. M., who will be specially glad to show you round, as you and she know each other already."

Brenda recognised dismissal, and stood up. Some parts of Miss Christopherson's

speech were a little damping somehow; she
didn't seem so absolutely sure as Brenda
would have expected that here at all events
she was going to be a first-class success.
She had had quite enough of playing second
fiddle in Nystrea; she wasn't sure that she
enjoyed having her inferiority to Margaret
Reresby pointed out with such unvarnished
plainness. It was quite a relief when M. M.
arrived.

She came in quite quietly, with the
orthodox tap at the door; but she jumped
when she saw Brenda standing beside the
Chesterfield.

" Hullo! Are you the Prin — the new
girl ? " she cried, and turned red.

Miss Christopherson smiled graciously.
" You will put Brenda in the way of every-
thing to start with, I know," she said. " She
will be in the bedroom with you and
Katharine. I shall see you again at prayers,
Brenda."

And Brenda found herself dismissed.

" That's a funny business," opined M. M.
outside the Principal's door. " I thought
this blessed Princess that's coming would be
no end of a grandee, and she just turns out
to be you."

" I don't see anything funny about it,"

Brenda remarked huffily. "You advised me to try and get here this term——"

"And you've got," M. M. concluded for her. "Well, it is funny, you know. I never thought you were a princess, or anything special; you seemed so very ordinary. I don't mean that rudely, you know; you're quite good-looking and all that," she added hastily. "But it was a pity you didn't tell us you were you—Bertram wouldn't have thought——"

Brenda didn't want to hear Bertram's uncomplimentary opinion all over again.

"I wish you would show me round," she said; "and I'd like to meet the girls I know, again—those two funny little things, and Margaret."

"You can see the kids if you want to let yourself down fussing after them," M. M. explained with candour; "but Margaret is in Sixth Form, and IVB's like me—and probably you—don't go pushing ourselves in there without an invite, I can tell you. I'll show you our room."

"Shall I be in IVB?" Brenda wanted to hear. "You can't know, can you?"

"Just a guess—you may be lower," M. M. said carelessly. "You've been taught at home, haven't you?"

Brenda felt extremely ruffled ; the attitude of school so far was very disconcerting. She decided not to answer ; that would be the best way of showing M. M. that she might be more polite. But M. M. chattered on, quite oblivious of offence.

" IVᴮ isn't a bad form, but Miss Kean is a beast ; got a down on me, too, and is killingly sarcastic half the time. However, p'raps she'll let loose on you if you come to us — and that will give me a rest."

A tall good-looking girl, with fair shingled hair, swung down the passage towards them.

" Thanks so much for the gorgeous roses, M. M.," she said pleasantly. " They were from you, weren't they ? "

" Yes, Miss Kean." M. M. looked rather awkward.

Miss Kean smiled and went on.

" That Miss Kean ? I thought you couldn't bear her," Brenda whispered.

" Oh, she isn't too bad always," M. M. said hastily. " Here's our dorm ; we get a decent view—right over to the sea."

" What's the big place with the tower ? "

" That's Rollincourt."

" Why, we're practically next door."

" I know. Bertram chucked us over some

roast chestnuts once over that wall and there was a row."

"My brother is there," Brenda said.

"The nice kid who was with you that day of the picnic?"

"Yes—Carol."

"What's it like being a princess?" M. M. wanted to know, though still in an off-hand way.

"Well, dullish."

"I should think it must be. Here's Katharine-Ursula. Hi, Katharine!"

Katharine, a fair, delicate-looking girl with shortsighted blue eyes, appeared in the doorway.

"This is Brenda, the new girl Miss Christopherson did all the palaver about," M. M. explained rapidly.

"What palaver?" Brenda wanted to know.

"Saying you were to be given a proper chance, because though foreign you couldn't help it," M. M. stated blandly.

Brenda walked towards the door, with her chin in the air. Katharine-Ursula caught hold of her and turned her round. Later on, Brenda was to learn that Katharine's shortsighted eyes could and did see more than most people's of the things that mattered.

" Don't you mind M. M.," she advised.
" They never paid twopence for her manners,
but she's comparatively harmless, and only
talks for the fun of it. Of course, Miss
Christopherson didn't say anything of the
kind; she just told us you were coming
from Nystrea."

Brenda felt a little soothed, especially as
M. M., probably by way of making amends,
gave her the choice of beds.

Matron appeared shortly, alert and capable
and determined, demanding Brenda's keys,
and informing her that her clothes would be
put away tidily and she would be required
to keep them so. Brenda assented languidly,
and getting rather bored by Matron's instructions to the other two, set out for a
little exploring on her own. She wasn't quite
sure that she was so eager for M. M. to show
her round after that last remark of hers.

She went downstairs and out into the
garden, avoiding Miss Christopherson's
private one, and skirting some big tennis
courts unoccupied at present, because nobody
had unpacked shoes as yet. Then she found
the high wall facing her, to which M. M. had
pointed when she told her of Bertram throwing the chestnuts over. Then she thought she
heard Carol's voice on the other side of it.

There was ivy on this side, and though Princess Brenda was not supposed to climb trees at home, it had not followed that she never did. She scrambled up with fair ease and landed herself atop of the wall.

" Hullo, Carol ! "

Carol was there, standing with a group of other grey flannel-suited boys, and looking so like the rest that Brenda found it quite difficult to pick him out.

" Hullo ! " she called again.

Carol looked up, and the other boys grinned a little awkwardly, while three or four took off their caps.

" It's my sister," Carol said, and ran up to the wall.

" Brenda, do go back ; we're not allowed to talk to the Beech House girls except when we meet them properly."

" You might be a little more grateful when I look in to see how you are," grumbled Brenda. " However——"

She was preparing to descend again on her own side when something very unforeseen occurred. A man's voice spoke sharply, " What are you doing ? " and he was only just in time to catch Brenda as she fell over —upon the Rollincourt side of the wall.

It was an undignified moment. Brenda

felt extremely annoyed with everything, and most of all with Carol for not being more enthusiastic about seeing her when she had taken such risks for him.

"Thank you very much for your prompt help," she said stiffly to the man who had caught her. "But you should be more careful about shouting suddenly; you startled me, and that was why I slipped."

"Well, I'm jiggered!" said the young man who had caught her. If to be jiggered is to look absolutely dumbfounded, that was certainly exactly what he was.

"Which is the way back to Beech House? I suppose my brother can show me?" Brenda inquired distantly, determined to have the word with Carol for which she had made such efforts.

The young man, who was big and clean and cheery-looking and very young, recovered himself a little.

"Look here," he said, "I suppose you are a new girl over there, and don't know the rules. But you take it from me that you'll get into no end of a row with your Head if you try on this little game again. If you've got twenty brothers over here, you mustn't come and see them,—except when it's allowed by your Head and ours.

Understand ? And what's more, you'll get your brother into trouble as well, and you'll probably think more of that than getting into a scrape yourself. I'm not going to take any notice this time—it hasn't happened—but it's never to happen again ! . . . And I suspect the best thing would be for me to boost you up, so that you can get back over the wall."

Brenda thought afterwards of several things she might have said. She was very much annoyed at having to be let off easily, so to speak, by a big, untidy young man, wearing a Norfolk jacket with belt hanging loose, and rather disreputable tennis shoes. But the warning about getting Carol into trouble had frightened her a little ; and she was on strange and unexpected ground. So she let the big young man lift her up till she could grip the top of the wall and scramble up, with the help of his shoulder, and got down on her own side of the wall with only a brief " Thank you."

No one was in view when she landed in the Beech House grounds, but when she rounded the corner and came on to the tennis courts, she nearly ran full tilt into Margaret Reresby, who was walking purposefully towards her, and looking less approachable than she had done at the picnic at home.

Brenda held out her hand, fully intending to say something pleasant, but Margaret did the talking before the new girl had time to make a remark, pleasant or otherwise.

" Why aren't you dressing for supper ? You've only five minutes, and if you lose a mark to B. House——"

She stopped. " Oh, you're a new girl; didn't some one tell you supper was at seven ? "

" I believe it was mentioned," Brenda said.

" Well, what do you suppose it was mentioned for ? To amuse the sparrows ? Attend to what's told you another time ; and now RUN ! "

Brenda ran. Margaret's tone was distinctly urgent, and she didn't seem to have the slightest idea of reminding Brenda that they had met before. Apparently the fact was of no interest.

Brenda arrived in her room with two minutes only remaining before the bell went, as an agitated M. M. and Katharine-Ursula informed her, in one reproachful breath— they were B. House as well, it seemed, whatever that might signify.

Though reproachful, they were very helpful, and Brenda was hustled out of her navy
frock between the pair of them well within
the time and into the old rose evening one
of an everyday Beech House evening. White
was reserved for concerts and other public
occasions by Miss Christopherson.

Brenda's hair must remain unbrushed and
tumbled, and as for her hands——

" Where on earth have you been to get
them in that mess ? " M. M. wanted to know.

Brenda waived the question ; she wasn't
exactly proud of the Rollincourt episode.
" I must wash," she said.

" You can't ; there's the bell," M. M.
assured her, with decision. " Rub your
hands on my sponge ; it's dampish, and
yours isn't unpacked—and come *along* ! "

Brenda came. She wasn't used to hustling,
and she found it very odd. In Nystrea,
whether at the Palace or at Castle Helsingfoss,
it was the business of somebody else to see
that the Princess was dressed in time, and
they saw to it. Here, Margaret, M. M., and
Katharine-Ursula all seemed to be of opinion
that she ought to have seen to that herself ;
and the help they had given was decidedly
of the rough - and - ready order. Brenda
hated to go down to a meal with rough hair

and unwashed hands, even though she had
often grumbled to Carol at the strict code
of tidiness prevailing at the Palace. But it
seemed as though her comfort was of no
importance in comparison with the prospect
of losing a mark to B. House. . . .

She sat next to M. M. at supper, and
M. M. was pleasant but off-hand. She gave
Brenda a good deal of information about
games and matches, and what was and
what was not played in the Summer Term,
but made none of the suggestions which
Brenda had expected as to the probability
that she might be in one of the teams.

After supper the girls filed into the big
hall, and Miss Christopherson read the school
rules in a clear voice that reached quite
easily to the back row of the girls, and spoke
of the coming term, then took prayers.

And in a very few minutes after that it
was bedtime for every one below IVA, and
the first day at Beech House was over.

Brenda went to sleep, feeling doubtful.

CHAPTER IV

THE RAFT ADVENTURE

BRENDA woke to brilliant sunshine and general cheerfulness. This three-bed room at Beech House was much sunnier and brighter than the big stately room which was hers at the Palace, — the room which had been slept in by the eldest Princess of the reigning House for generations.

In that room some of the furniture had been new when Brenda's great-great-aunt was a girl, but most of it dated back a good deal further. Brenda was very tired of the dim tambour-work of seats and curtains, of dull gilding, and, above all, of heaviness and what she described as " stodginess " ; and it was so delightful to have a room where air and sunshine came in freely, and there was everything that was necessary and nothing that was not, and, above all, other girls to talk to.

At the Palace everybody about her knew their place so dreadfully well, and even when, as very occasionally happened, two or three

carefully selected girls came to tea, they
had been reminded beforehand exactly how
they ought to behave, and they behaved.
There wasn't much spontaneity about the
talk at these times.

It was a real joy to be able to talk as she
got into the unfamiliar gym frock of school ;
and the talk was so interesting because it
was about things which she had never been
allowed to do.

It appeared that in England, as in Nystrea,
the spring had been extraordinarily hot, and
Miss Christopherson had held out hopes to
Margaret Reresby that bathing might begin
for swimmers, as the water would be so
exceptionally warm.

" We always do start earlier than other
schools, only we aren't allowed long in
the water, and we've got to keep going
hard," M. M. explained. " Can you swim,
Brenda ? "

" Oh yes." Brenda was sure of that.
She had been taught to swim when she was
five, and went into the private swimming
bath at the Palace three times a week
through all the winter, with a swimming
mistress in the water with her, and a trained
nurse watching from the tessellated pave-
ment to make sure she wasn't blue-lipped

or over-tired, and her maid standing in her private bathing cabin, mounting guard over two enormous towels kept warm on hot pipes. " I've done a lot of swimming," she added.

" Good ! Then you may be of some use for the ' Cup,' " M. M. told her encouragingly. " We were very near getting it last year, but our best diver has left, worse luck. If we get bathing leave to-day, speak up, and ask if you may go, and we'll see if you're any good."

Again that dubious tone about her powers. Brenda would not show that she did not like it, but she was determined to display what she could do in the swimming line, and then perhaps M. M. would realise that this new girl at least was entitled to a higher place in the school world than the other girls seemed willing to give her.

" You're not a delicate, are you ? " Katharine-Ursula wanted to know.

" I'm sure I'm not."

" That's a good thing. Then you may be allowed to go out to the raft," M. M. said. " But that's only for really good swimmers, you know ; it's a fair way out."

Brenda was, of course, instantly determined to swim out to that raft this very morning if bathing were allowed at all. But she didn't say so. It would be better to do it first, considering the rather doubtful attitude held by everybody towards a new girl's powers.

Sure enough Miss Christopherson came in at the end of breakfast and made an announcement.

She had received a good report on the warmth of the water from Miss Kington. All girls who had passed Miss Kington's swimming test might down go with her at twelve o'clock for the shortest possible bathe, but no one must be more than five minutes in the water. She trusted the girls to keep moving all the time, and not to give her any cause to regret having allowed them to begin practising for the " Cup " so unusually early.

" Thank you very much, Miss Christopherson.   We'll be ever so careful," promised Margaret Reresby for the school.

Brenda uplifted her voice : " Miss Christopherson ! "

M. M., her neighbour, poked her sharply. " Stand up when you speak to Miss Christopherson."

Brenda stood, scarlet with annoyance, at the very public admonition.   M. M. might at least have whispered it. The girl on her other side was grinning most objectionably.

" I don't know what Miss Kington's test is, but I have passed endless tests and swum for years at home. I suppose I may join the bathing party this morning ? I should like very much to do so."

The whole table listened with flattering attention. You could have heard a pin drop. Miss Christopherson did not answer Brenda's little speech for what seemed like a very long quarter of a minute. Then she spoke, slowly and consideringly :

" You are quite new to school life, Brenda, and of course do not quite understand rules and arrangements and other things. Ordinarily I should not allow a girl to bathe until our conditions have been complied with, but if Miss Kington will be so good as to watch your swimming for a moment or so, I will take it that you are up to our standard and allow you to bathe with the experts this morning."

It was borne in upon Brenda that Miss Christopherson was doing her a favour. She said, " Thank you very much," and sat down again.

" Lucky brute ! " whispered M. M. " I thought you would get your head bitten off for cheek."

" Why ? " thought the bewildered Brenda, but did not ask it.

Twelve o'clock found twenty happy people, carrying bathing dresses and towels, racing at breakneck pace down the steep private path to the beach.

Under the cliff the eight little bathing huts belonging to the school stood nestled comfortably. Out on a glorious blue rippling sea swayed the raft of which Brenda had heard so much. She looked at it critically as she undressed in one of the huts with two other girls. It didn't look too far out. She hoped very much that Miss Kington wouldn't waste much of her time over that silly test, for somehow or another she meant to get out to that raft and show M. M. and Margaret Reresby what this new girl could do in the swimming line !

It was a full minute after the other girls had rushed, shouting and laughing, down the shelving beach to the sea, that Brenda was ready to follow them. She wasn't very used to doing everything for herself as yet.

The girls were all in the water by the time she reached Miss Kington, and Miss Kington, instead of waiting patiently to see her pass her test, was in the water herself, helping M. M. with side-stroke.

Brenda waited, in growing indignation,

for perhaps a quarter of a minute, then she called, " Are you ready, Miss Kington ? "

But the girls were making so much noise that it was hardly wonderful Miss Kington did not hear her; and all the precious minutes were being wasted, Brenda felt.

After all, that swimming test was purely a form in her case; and if she waited any longer, there wouldn't be a chance of getting out to the raft and back in the time. Brenda didn't wait any longer, but plunged into the water, and swam with great strokes towards the raft. She would soon show the rest that this new girl was not out to play second fiddle in the swimming line at least.

She thought she heard a call behind her, but couldn't be sure of it; and as everybody of the Beech House party was laughing and shouting, not to mention a troop of boys, who were enjoying themselves in the water and making even more noise about the business, it was not surprising that she could not distinguish her name.

Swimming at top speed with her eyes fixed on the raft, she collided with a girl who was swimming in, on her back, and swimming rather unskilfully. Both went under, and swallowed more water than was pleasant; but Brenda was too good a swimmer to mind. She came up laughing, but the other girl didn't seem too happy, and floundered a good deal in the effort to turn over on her front.

Brenda trod water and steadied her. "Sorry, but you went into me, I think," she remarked.

The girl was recovering. "I dare say I did. Apologies and all that. I'm all right now, but I'm not much of a swimmer. Are you coming in? Swim in with me, do."

"I'm going out to the raft," Brenda explained civilly.

"*Are* you? I wish I were! I can't, except at low tide, and then it's no fun," the girl said.

Brenda looked her over. She wasn't very big or heavy. She herself had held her up with the greatest ease while she was breathless and choking and very helpless with the sudden douche.

"If you like to put your hands on my shoulders and lie out, I'll take you there," she suggested.

"You couldn't, could you?"

"Of course I could. It's the easiest thing in the world for any one who can swim," Brenda explained. "Just lie out, and I'll do all the rest."

The girl, whose name, she explained, was
Peggy, agreed joyfully, though with a slight
tremor in her voice, which might have been
due to either cold or nervousness. But
Brenda of Nystrea had had so little to do
with other girls that she wasn't educated
up to shades of tone from people who would
never have owned fear in so many words,
and she and Peggy set off for the raft—
Brenda with a comfortable feeling at the
back of her mind that now at last she was
showing how she could swim.

As a matter of fact it wasn't quite as easy
as she expected to swim the distance to the
raft with Peggy clinging to her shoulders.
She had often enough swum in this way with
her swimming instructress, who was considerably bigger than Peggy; but then Miss
Wrankin was not in the least nervous, and
two fingers of a perfect swimmer laid lightly
upon your shoulders by way of a test are
quite a different proposition from a tight
clutch by a person who isn't particularly
happy or sure that you won't let her in.

And then the sea, even at the end of two
months of unclouded sunshine, is not very
warm at the end of April; not nearly as
warm as the carefully warmed private baths
belonging to the Palace; and the cold and

Peggy's weight together were inclined to
shorten her breath. Brenda wouldn't give
up what she had undertaken to do; her
pride revolted at the idea — but she was
beginning to realise that it would take a good
deal longer than five minutes to get to the
raft and back, with Peggy in it too.

She was certainly swimming lower in the
water, and Peggy got a swallow and gasped
and clutched tighter and more heavily and
half dropped her feet.

" Don't do that ! " Brenda said sharply.
She did not let herself think how thankful
she would be to reach the raft ; Peggy was
growing most uncommonly heavy.

" We're almost there," she gasped out.
" When I say, ' Now ! ' let go and tread
water, while I get up on the raft ; then I'll
give you a hand on."

" Ye—s," faltered Peggy, with chattering
teeth, " but I can't t—tread water properly,
you know."

" Well, swim then," Brenda told her impatiently ; " I can't get hold with you hanging
to me like this."

The raft was looming above them, a good
deal above them, to say truth. It was raised
on barrels that stood right up out of the deep
green water, a fact which Brenda had not

realised when she saw it from afar. It was rolling too, more than was quite agreeable, for the wind was freshening, and the waves were not so tiny now, as Brenda had been finding to her cost during the last few minutes of her swim.

A bigger wave than she had met before came upon her unexpectedly, while she was trying to see on which side of the raft there were the usual steps. She missed her stroke, and Peggy screamed and clutched wildly at her arm.

Brenda made a drowning grasp at the raft with her free hand and missed it—and then she seemed to herself to be all tangled up with Peggy under a mountain of green water, and, for the first time since she had begun to swim, was horribly afraid.

She tried to kick out, to free herself to some extent; if only she could get herself and Peggy to the raft, they could wait there for help. But though her efforts brought them to the surface for a moment, it was to discover the alarming fact that they were now considerably farther off the raft than when Peggy had downed her. Her struggles seemed to have taken the pair of them quite in the wrong direction, and Peggy had both her arms in a clutch of desperation.

Probably, if Brenda could have forced herself to keep calm, and tread water hard, she might have kept up till help came; but Peggy was still struggling, and seemed to have grown abnormally big and heavy, and Brenda was continually going under. . . .

Far off she saw the green cap worn by Miss Kington, bobbing towards her. Miss Kington was coming, but she was going— right under now !—and sheer absolute panic had seized her, taking away nearly all the sense she possessed. . . . This was drowning . . . and then a voice that was oddly familiar spoke behind her—spoke urgently and loudly :

" Kick off—I'll hold her ! "

Brenda was almost past recognising Carol or feeling any surprise that he should be there. She only knew vaguely that he caught cleverly at Peggy, as the two struggling girls came within his reach, and, treading water furiously, managed to hold her up, and at the full length of his stiffened arms, to keep her from pulling him down.

" Get to the raft," he panted, and Brenda had just sense and strength to strike out blindly for it, and catch weakly at a submerged rung of the little ladder to one side. She got a little breath back and turned round, swinging with the swing of the raft, and becoming conscious of everything again.

How in the world would Carol manage ? —Carol, who was not nearly so strong a swimmer as herself ? She had left him to the rescuing of Peggy, who, for all the goodness of her swimming, had very nearly drowned her. Brenda, who was very fond of her only brother, felt a sudden dreadful pang of fear for him.

But to her intense surprise she saw that he seemed to be managing better than she had done. Somehow he was keeping Peggy up and at arm's length.

And he had not to hold on for more than a quarter of a minute after Brenda looked round. Two swimmers were converging rapidly upon him—the green head and a shock brown one, belonging to a big young man, who was farther away than Miss Kington was, but reached the boy first.

He took Peggy's head between his hands and swam on his back towards the raft, keeping a wary eye on Carol, whose swimming powers seemed nearly exhausted.

Miss Kington came straight to Brenda, and spoke quietly and steadily : " Get up on to the raft at once, Brenda ; I will help you."

Far from scorning the help, Brenda was thankful for it. It had seemed a physical impossibility to do more than cling to that rung and just keep her head above the water by that means. She felt weak and shaky and very cold, and crouched, shivering, in a huddled heap upon the raft, above the barrels, while first Peggy, then Carol, then Miss Kington, and, last of all, the young man joined her there. And in the last named, as he climbed up and shook himself like a great water dog, Brenda was beyond measure disgusted to recognise her unceremonious and plain-spoken acquaintance of yesterday, the big young master of Carol's school.

She felt that she had not fulfilled her ambition and landed on the raft precisely in the way, and with the company, she would have chosen!

CHAPTER V

A HELPING HAND

THE young man did not seem to recognise Brenda ; that was a comfort,
though certainly surprising to her.   But then
he was very busy.

" Better get the whole lot in by boat,
hadn't we ? " he remarked bluntly to Miss
Kington, and signalled vigorously to a boat
which was being pulled by a blue-jerseyed
person, not far away.   Miss Kington, busy
with the sobbing Peggy, just nodded agree-
ment.

" And I hope that Miss Christopherson will
give it to these two, HOT ! " the young man
added quite ferociously, when he had succeeded in attracting the boatman's attention
to his needs.

Brenda could hardly believe that the wish
applied to her.   " Peggy isn't anything to do
with Miss Christopherson," she explained, as
well as she could, between chattering teeth.
" We just met in the water."

" And were precious near being drowned.

Lucky for you this chap had a little more sense than you have," grunted the young man, with an encouraging slap to Carol's shoulder; and Brenda realised suddenly, and with immense disgust, that here she was playing second fiddle to Carol again.

Carol did say, " Oh, Brenda had the worst of it before I came," but nobody took any particular notice of the remark, or seemed to think for a moment that it had needed an uncommonly good swimmer to bring another girl out so far, or that it was Peggy's panic, not Brenda's inadequacy, which had landed them in a predicament where Carol's help was needed.

She went back to shore in an offended silence, which lasted while Miss Kington, rubbing her uncomfortably hard with a very rough towel in her bathing cabin, informed her just exactly what she thought about her conduct.

Brenda found her voice again in angry self-defence. " I assure you, Miss Kington, there wouldn't have been the smallest danger about the business if Peggy had only shown a little sense. . . ."

" You mean if *you* had," Miss Kington told her brutally. " You behaved idiotically as well as very wrongly, Brenda."

Brenda, who was accustomed to having her faults pointed out in a more considerate manner by her instructors, stiffened with indignation.

" I have often taken people—at least one person, my swimming mistress—for a bigger distance on my shoulders," she explained, " and I am an experienced swimmer."

" I dare say, but that has nothing to do with it. You were told to come to me before you started, and you didn't, and because of that bit of disobedience—which must be reported to Miss Christopherson, of course—you got the chance of doing a thing which I should have thought silly even for a ten-year-old. You ought to have known that not the most experienced swimmer in the world finds it easy to deal with a panicky clutch, and you didn't show half as much sense when you had that danger to face as the little boy from Rollincourt."

Brenda was too much disgusted to answer that ; was she never to be anything but second fiddle, even here ? The impression she had made so far seemed quite of the wrong kind.

And her interview with Miss Christopherson did not tend to cheer her. Miss Christopherson was very grave indeed, not so much about the dreadful consequences which had so nearly followed on Brenda's attempt to demonstrate the goodness of her swimming, but on the cause. She drew from the reluctant Brenda the fact that she had known it was disobedient not to go first to Miss Kington, but had thought it quite unnecessary for so good a swimmer to pass any test, and that she had gone out to the raft to show the rest that she would be of use for the "Cup."

Miss Christopherson did not dwell upon the danger of the whole proceeding, but said something which struck Brenda, though she did not like it.

"If you will look into your motives with absolute honesty, I think you will find that a good deal of conceit was at the bottom of it all, my dear," she said. "You thought yourself above our Beech House rules, and you wanted, as the girls would say, to show off. . . ."

"I wanted to help in winning the 'Cup,'" murmured Brenda, not feeling particularly proud of herself.

"Very likely, but I think you will find that the other motive was the driving force behind an action which might quite easily have drowned two people—possibly a third, your brother Carol. Now, Brenda, you will one day occupy a position of importance, when what you say and do will influence many people. You have to be more particular than other girls, not less, to fit yourself for the bigger school of life, by learning what Beech House is meant to teach you. I must punish you for your disobedience. You will take a conduct mark, and that loses five marks to your house—B."

Brenda woke up. " Oh, please don't do that—the other girls will hate it so," she pleaded. " I'm sorry about this morning, Miss Christopherson. I was wrong, but please give me a punishment that the others won't know about."

" That is my rule for wilful disobedience," Miss Christopherson said gravely. " B. House must lose the five marks, Brenda. That will do. Go and get ready for luncheon."

Brenda was too proud to beg any more, even if there had not been finality in Miss Christopherson's voice. She went to wash her hands for luncheon, feeling thoroughly depressed ; but of course she wasn't going to let the other girls see that. So she hummed a tune quite jauntily, as she went to the big ground-floor dressing-room, with its rows of white washing-basins and well-polished taps.

"Hullo! you seem pretty pleased with yourself," M. M. said, looking up from her basin. "You got off with a lecture, then, on account of your newness, I suppose?"

"No; I have a conduct mark, whatever that may mean exactly," Brenda said.

"*What?*" shrieked M. M., "a conduct mark! Five off for B. House, Brenda!"

"Well, I am sorry about it," Brenda said; "but, though it turned out unluckily I admit, I was really trying to lend you a hand with your Swimming Cup."

Brenda's tone was more airy than it would otherwise have been, because she was trying so hard to keep her end up after her rather depressing interview with Miss Christopherson. But the other girls, particularly the B. House girls, could hardly be expected to know that, and Margaret Reresby's answer was crushing:

"You had better have the sense to keep the rules, if you want to be of use, and leave the swimming-cup arrangements to your seniors."

Brenda felt quite as annihilated as when her father made one of his sarcastic corrections. Somehow she couldn't find anything to say.

It was borne in upon her that she was making an impression of quite the wrong kind at Beech House.

．　　．　　．　　．　　．　　．

There was prep from 2.30 to 4.30; in the Summer Term the Beech House girls had their free time from tea onwards.

Brenda did not find the work she had to do particularly difficult, but she was teased by the sense of the other people in the room. Pages rustled, pencil-boxes rattled, there was a scratching of many pens, and every sound was distracting.

Her dull, solid schoolroom at the Palace was, at least, very quiet during lesson-hours. Miss Heron sat by, while she did her prep, ready to answer any necessary questions; and no one else was in the room at all. It was distinctly muddling to be one of so many, and to add to her troubles she was extremely tired after her long swim and fright of the morning. Her prep got on very slowly indeed, and at the back of her mind there was a haunting fear that, if she worked more slowly than the other girls, she would be put into a lower form at once. It would be too humiliating to find herself below her contemporaries, intellectually!

The thought did not help her at all, for

she promptly made two careless mistakes in her French translation, and had to tear out the page and rewrite it.

The mistress who was taking prep for three forms, put her head in at IVB classroom. "Five-and-twenty past four; put everything away tidily," she said, and there was a stretching, an opening of desks, and a hasty shovelling in of exercise - books, pencil-cases, etc., pell-mell.

"Thanks be!" ejaculated M. M., as she tapped Brenda on the shoulder. "Come along; we have tea at half-past."

"I haven't finished; I'll drop tea, I think," Brenda said.

"Rubbish! you can't. If you haven't finished, you must just give in that you haven't," M. M. explained, laying hands on her exercise-book.

"Please leave my things alone. I shall get on much faster when I have the place to myself," Brenda told her, with decision.

The rest of the form had gone, with the exception of Katharine - Ursula. M. M. turned to her. "She can't stay, can she, K.?"

"Look here, Brenda, you shut shop now— you mayn't be away from tea without leave, you know," Katharine explained, in her sensible way. "But I'll ask Miss Kean if you may have twenty minutes after tea, for once, as you're so new, and then I'll see if I can be a help when we're by ourselves. It must be worrying to work in a crowd when you're not used to it."

"Thanks ever so much," Brenda said. She really was grateful for a little sympathy.

Miss Kean said, "Well, this once; but it mustn't be a precedent, Brenda," and Brenda and Katharine-Ursula retired to IVB as soon as tea was over, on the understanding that only twenty minutes longer might be spent indoors.

Tea and the break had helped, and all went swimmingly, Katharine reading out the figures in Brenda's scribbled sums for her to copy, hearing her read over the English poetry, and advising on the outline map where countries must be filled in.

The poetry wasn't quite word perfect by the time the twenty minutes ended, but Katharine thought it would soak into Brenda's memory before the morning, and if she got up fairly punctually she could have another look at it before breakfast.

"I'm ever so grateful. I don't know why you've been so nice to me," Brenda said, as they put things away.

"Oh, that's nothing," Katharine assured her. "Everybody means to be all right to you, you know. You mustn't mind M. M.'s blunt way."

"I don't, only I'm sorry about those five marks."

"Every one gets a conduct mark sometimes," Katharine remarked consolingly. "Margaret wouldn't have been half so down on you about it, only she thought you didn't care much—and every one gets keen on their House. You will."

Brenda wasn't so sure about that, with Margaret as House Captain, but she didn't say so. Life at Nystrea had been a training in the art of holding one's tongue.

"Cheer up!" Katharine concluded, "and come out. You must get into one of the tennis sets and put all the bothers out of your head."

"Aren't you going to play?" Brenda asked, as the two made their way out into the sunny garden.

"I'm going to coach some new girls, who want to be Guides, for the Tenderfoot."

"Do you have Guides here? Oh, I remember M. M. said so that afternoon at the picnic, when I met her. I think I'd like to be one."

Katharine looked pleased. " I wish you would. We've a ripping Company here; more than three-quarters of the school are Guides."

" And do you teach them to be Guides ? "

" I help my own Patrol—I'm a Patrol Leader."

" What's that ? " Brenda wanted to know.

" You don't have Guides in Nystrea, I expect ? A Patrol Leader is a sort of non-commissioned officer. Six or eight Guides go to a Patrol, and all wear the same emblem and shoulder-knot and belong. We have our Guide meeting on Saturday morning. You can come along and see for yourself if you like."

" Can't I come now ? "

" Yes, if you want, of course you can. But this will be nothing showy, just two new juniors learning Guide Law and Guide Signs, and the first principles of drill and so on."

" I'll come, if you don't mind," Brenda persisted. Katharine's company was soothing after the various reverses of the day, and she was inclined to share in her interests just then, whatever they might be.

They found the two new juniors waiting in a quiet corner of the grounds at the angle of the Rollincourt wall, both very busy with bits of stout string.

" How are the knots getting on ? "
Katharine asked. " A Tenderfoot wants to
know four," she added, for Brenda's benefit.

" The ' reef's ' all right," remarked Sonia,
the smaller of the two, " but the ' middleman ' stumps me. Do say your rhyme again
about it, Katharine."

Katharine laughed. " It's only to re-
mind you which knot you're making—that's
right, Nancy ; a slip knot there—and there,
so that the loop between will stay the same
size without giving, and remember :

" ' " The Middleman " acquires its name from the guides
    of the mountain-sides ;
It is used to safeguard the Middle man, who travels
    between two guides.' "

" Let me try," Brenda asked, sitting down
beside the other two.

" Better start with a reef," advised
Katharine. " Here, these two bits of string
are of exactly equal thickness. Don't make
it into a granny knot now ! "

" How shall I know a granny ? " Brenda
wanted to know.

" Easy enough : a granny comes undone
when you pull it ; a reef gets tighter. I'll
show you, and then I'll tell you the ten
points of the Guide Law, the Law that every
Tenderfoot must know and understand,

because it's the heart of it all—at least that's how our Captain explains it."

Brenda listened attentively, while Katharine repeated the Guide Law, that very comprehensive Law which every Guide pledges herself to do her best to keep. It came over her that it was a finer code than the strict rule prevailing at home: " A Princess must not——"

Here every point of the Law began : " A Guide is——" ; it took for granted that the Guide was out for something better than just being told not to do this and that.

" I'd like to be a Guide. I'll be a Guide, and in your Patrol," Brenda said impulsively to Katharine, but was rather badly damped by her answer.

" I hope you will be, but you'll have a month to think about it—and no one can be enrolled till they have attended their four Company meetings, and passed their Tenderfoot. And the Captain settles which Patrol you join."

Perhaps Katharine realised that she had been a little depressing, for she added quickly, " But I'd love to have you in my Patrol ; we're the Swallows. All our Company have bird emblems for the Patrols."

" Who else is in yours ? " Brenda asked.

"Peggy Wantage—she's IVB; her desk was two from yours on the left," Katharine explained; "and Sanna Moore—you sat next her at tea. You wouldn't have noticed Poppy Hendleton or Judy Kerne; they're both IIIA. Mary Grantly is older than we are, but then she joined the Guides late; and M. M. is my second."

"M. M.!" Brenda was not at all pleased at that news. "Is she in your Patrol?"

"Rather! We joined the Guides together, and have always been in the same Patrol ever since."

"What does it mean to be a second?"

"She takes command when the P.L. isn't there, and helps her always."

"Then she's a sort of leader, too?"

"Oh yes."

"Well, I'll think about being a Guide," Brenda said cautiously. She wasn't at all sure how she would like being under the orders of M. M. "Thank you so much for letting me come and learn about Guiding, though," she added.

It was an odd sensation, being grateful to some one for companioning her, but it had been borne in upon Princess Brenda of Nystrea that her first day at Beech House had not been an unqualified success.

CHAPTER VI

GUIDES ON PARADE

BY Saturday morning Brenda was beginning to feel a little more at home in her new surroundings. The classical master had praised her construing publicly in the Latin class; Peggy Wantage had walked with her in the croc and made no allusion to marks lost to B. House. She asked questions about Nystrea, and Brenda found it rather soothing to talk of home.

M. M. was still rather a trial, but Katharine—K. or Katharine-Ursula in full, for some obscure reason to her friends—was particularly nice and helpful, and she made up for a great deal.

Brenda hadn't made up her mind whether to go to the Guide Parade as a prospective Guide or not when Saturday morning saw Katharine and M. M. putting on their Guide kit as they got up; but when ten o'clock struck, and the P.L.'s filed out from the Court of Honour, held in Sixth Form, and Margaret Reresby, Company Leader, blew her whistle

sharply, she was among the ten new girls
in gym frocks who followed the uniforms
into the School Hall at the double.

The Guide Captain, Miss Ferrars, a stranger
to Brenda because she was not on the Staff,
desired all the Guides to sit in Horseshoe,
as soon as the whole Company had greeted
her entrance by coming smartly to attention, and saluting with commendable precision at the command of Miss Kean,
Lieutenant.

Brenda had seen too many reviews to be
surprised by the precision with which nearly
eighty girls came to attention ; what did
surprise her was the sudden change from the
formality of the salute to the elder-sisterish
direction, " Sit, Guides," and the easy way
in which the Captain sat herself down, cross-
legged, in the midst of the Horseshoe, saying,
" Now to talk over our term's programme,
and to find out where new Guides want to go."

It was difficult to imagine such an attitude
or tone among the officials of the Palace, or
the Household Troops. But the Guides of
Beech House appeared to take the sudden
change quite as a matter of course.

The term's programme seemed to include
many exciting things, Brenda thought ; there
was a Shield to be competed for with other

Companies, and there was plenty of fun over the discussions of how the work for it should be tackled. Any Guide who liked seemed to be allowed to offer suggestions; quite small girls seemed bursting with ideas. The Company seemed like one large-sized family, where every one was keen upon the same things.

When the " Open Parliament," as it seemed that this section of the first Guide meeting was called, came to a cheerful ending, Miss Ferrars asked the new girls whether they would like to work and play with the Company for a month, and then make the decision whether to be enrolled as Guides or not.

" And, let me see, Brenda, it is you who are in a room with Katharine and Mariota; would you like to be placed provisionally with the Swallows ? " asked the Captain. And Brenda answered " Yes," before she had really decided whether she could bear to be under M. M.'s orders. However, it was only for a month—any one could stick anything or a month, she thought ; if she couldn't do with M. M. for a second, she needn't be enrolled as a Guide at all.

The places of the new girls settled, the Captain rose to her feet. There was a

vigorous scraping of shoes on the floor as
over eighty girls got up in a hurry at the
same moment. Then the Captain blew her
whistle, and everybody stiffened to stillness
and an instantaneous startling silence, into
which rang out Miss Ferrars' voice, all
Captain now, " Leaders—fall in ! "

Brenda watched with interest as the ten
Patrol Leaders doubled forward, and fell in,
one long line before Miss Ferrars, Margaret
exactly opposite to her, five paces distant.

" Leaders—attention ! "

" Leaders—number ! "

" To the right, to two paces—extend ! "

" Company—on parade—fall *in* ! "

Brenda was behindhand there; for she
was so absorbed in watching, that she forgot
that " Company " included herself, at least
provisionally. She landed at the end of the
Swallow Patrol in a scramble and distinctly
flustered; but none of the new Guides were
too sure about their method of falling in,
and she, at least, had the advantage of the
others in knowing the meaning of " Right
dress." Inspection followed, and then
" Roll " was taken, after which the Company
divided into sections for twenty minutes of
stern and strenuous work.

Miss Ferrars had a class of fourteen

senior Guides on the First-Aid Badge;
Katharine and the A. House Captain,
Marcelle Thomson, coached in second-class
work; while Miss Kean passed Guides in
three out of the second-class subjects—
signalling the Morse Alphabet, making a
bed, and the elementary First Aid of the
second class. Outside on the Hard Court
a squad of thirty, juniors and beginners,
learned how to fall in, number, right dress,
right, left, and about turn; and form fours,
without making a long leg and scooping
themselves into the correct place. Brenda
was with this section, and found the drill
interesting, though less easy than it looked.
She was twice picked out for praise by
Margaret Reresby, and that was pleasant,
though she had not quite forgiven Margaret
for her ruthless snubbing.

It began to drizzle; the glorious weather
had broken at last, and this Saturday
morning was dull and chilly. Margaret
halted her squad, explained exactly what
should be done on the word "Dismiss!"
gave it, and fell them in again, rain and all,
because four had not attended and gone wrong
in the salute. Then she gave out a notice:

"Guides, go straight to your Patrol
corners."

Brenda followed Nancy and Sonia; the phrase " Patrol corners " was Greek to her, but she thought they might know. And in one corner of the gym she saw that a large and triumphant banner had been planted since the half-hour of Physical Drill with which the morning had started. It was a banner made of blue glazed calico, with an appliquéd border of blue-and-white swallows all flying towards a great golden sun with diffuse rays. Below the legend, in bold black letters : " *Swallows seek Sunshine.*"

" That's our Patrol corner ; decent, isn't it ? " Nancy remarked. " Isn't the banner beautiful ? M. M. made it ; she's frightfully clever. Don't you like our motto ? K. made that up ; I jolly well think it's the nicest motto of all the Patrols ; K. says it means we've got to look for the sunshine in everything—has she told you that ? "

" No," Brenda said, rather amused. " I expect she keeps those sorts of remarks for you younger ones."

" You're all the same in Guides, unless you're a P.L. or second ; and you're only a Tenderfoot, same as I am, and you weren't a Brownie before, either—so there ! " Nancy flared in wrath, which was rather surprising to Brenda, who couldn't see what she had said to offend her. However, they were in the Patrol corner by that time, so there was no more talk.

Katharine wasn't there; probably she was still busy with the second-class work; but M. M. was taking on the instructions of the Patrol, in a capable manner that impressed Brenda, though rather against her will. The idea seemed to be that the whole Patrol should try to pass the Fireman's Badge, the examination for which came so near the end of the term that there would be at least a reasonable chance of the three new Guides being through their second class before they need send in their names.

" A Patrol Badge like that is so topping to have," M. M. explained. " We can have it on our Patrol Flag, you know, as well as wearing it individually; and it's so jolly to be all working for the same; besides, it's such a useful badge to have, and keeps us from losing our heads in a fire, if it happens. The only thing is, it means uncommonly stiff work for the three new Guides to get through their second class in only a little over six weeks."

" But why not leave the second class till we're through this Patrol Badge ? " suggested Brenda helpfully ; but M. M. shook her head.

" No go, Brenda ; you mayn't put in for a Proficiency Badge till you have your second class. Guide rules."

M. M. wasn't in the least snubby now, though Brenda had said the wrong thing. Brenda thought she liked her better as a Guide than in ordinary life. " Oh, well, I don't mind working hard," she promised, quite forgetting that she had not at all made up her mind that she intended to be a Guide at all. But then the Patrol in general were so keen on the Fireman's Badge, and enthusiasm is, luckily, quite as catching as depression.

M. M. proceeded to begin instructing on the badge, which she wore among the six that already went in neat pairs up the left sleeve of her navy Guide jumper.

" I'm no good at lecturing," she explained ; " but I know what the examiners wanted me to know when I took the badge last year. We shall have to finish our coaching for it at the fire station, but I can tell you the beginning."

And tell she did, in vigorous and rather slangy diction, for the ten minutes that remained of Patrol time, and got a most creditable amount of useful information in, too.

Brenda learned that when you saw a little smoke where it shouldn't be, it wasn't the right thing for a Guide to rush straight to the fire station, and turn out firemen and engines, but to find out first whether it was a little smoulder in a tool shed that you could put out yourself with a half-bucket of water.

She learned that in a real fire the first thing for a Guide to do, after ringing up the fire station, was to help in saving first life, then property. She learned that there is a right and a wrong way of going about in a house on fire; that a Guide with her head screwed on straight shuts doors and windows behind her, because draughts feed a fire; and that where smoke is rolling and choking there is always a current of air near the floor, so the Guide should go on her hands and knees. She learned that a wet handkerchief tied round your mouth is good, and that a wet blanket, if not too large and cumbersome, is better still, because it will protect your head and body when the flames are too near. She learned how to drag an insensible person, too heavy for you to carry, to a window, and how to get her across

your shoulders and on to a ladder. She
learned that an oil or electric fire should not
be put out with water but with earth or
ashes, because flaming oil will spread out on
the top of water, and water is a conductor
of electricity. And the Captain's whistle
shrilled out most annoyingly, just as Brenda
was crawling after M. M., her handkerchief
across her mouth (supposed to be soaking),
in a daring attempt to rescue Nancy, who
lay, snoring horribly, on the vaulting horse,
representing her bed.

"Bother!" Brenda muttered. She was
beginning to recognise that whistle, and
knew that Guides ran at once when they
heard it.

All round the gym, and in the classrooms
next it, Patrol work was stopping on the
instant. Bits of string were stuffed back
into pockets; Guide ties, which had been
used for triangular bandages, were being
replaced by their owners at the double.
M. M., with the help of Nancy and Judy
Kerne, pushed back the horse to its proper
place; then followed the stream of Guides
doubling for the School Hall.

Brenda was beside Peggy Wantage. "I
liked that Badge talk," she said. "M. M.
knows a lot, doesn't she?"

" Rather ! " Peggy agreed. " We're no
end lucky to get such a topping P.L. and
second."

" I suppose M. M. will be a leader soon,
as she's so good ? " Brenda suggested.

" Don't suppose so ; she and K. are the
same age ; they'll leave together, most
likely."

" Do you mean she'll always be only a
second ? "

" What's wrong with that ? " Peggy asked,
in genuine surprise. " Of course she will,
unless she leaves her Patrol. Guides do
that now and then, but not often. And
M. M. won't ; she's too keen on the
Swallows."

It was a new idea to Brenda that people
might be content with the second place.
" But it's different in Guides," she thought,
as she obeyed Miss Ferrars' ringing order—
" Patrols in file at far end of hall."

" What is going to happen ? " Brenda
whispered to Peggy Wantage.

" Some new stunt, I expect ; the weather's
knocked out tracking, which was what we
meant to do," Peggy whispered back. " But
it's sure to be something topping ; Miss
Ferrars always thinks of jolly unexpected
things to do."

" We have to revise our programme for
this meeting," the Captain said pleasantly ;
" but we don't mean it to be a worse
one for that.   Patrol Leaders, forward !
Stand here at this end of the hall, but
place yourselves so that none of you face
your own Patrols.   That's right.   We
are going to give the seconds a grand
opportunity of showing what they can
do."

Subdued groans were heard from the
seconds, headed by M. M.   " These ten
envelopes upon the table will be handed in
a moment, one to each Patrol.   The contents
are the same in each.   The seconds will have
to decide how to deal with them, and there
are now twenty minutes to the moment when
I shall call them in.   We will see which
Patrol scores highest.   Leaders, hand the
envelopes to the seconds facing you, and
then come back to me."

M. M. tore the envelope apart, her Patrol
crowding round her in acute anxiety to know
what it might be.   Inside were the following
contents, certainly unexpected :

    I. A small square of stuff, with a linen
       button fixed to it by a threaded
       needle.

II. A slip of paper on which was written :

> A Kingfisher.
> A Water Wagtail.
> A Fox.
> A Fieldmouse.
> A Beetle.
> A Dragon Fly.

" Describe each of these to the P.L. facing you, without using their name. Ten marks will be given for the Leader who guesses all within three minutes. Five marks for four minutes. Two for five. Nothing after."

III. Two pieces of electric wire, with frayed-out ends.

IV. A square of paper, with a pencil and a red and blue chalk. " Draw and colour the Union Jack."

V. One member of the Patrol go to her room and pack her suit-case for the week-end. Suit-case when packed to be brought to the P.L. facing her Patrol.

VI. One member of each Patrol to prepare to receive a Morse message from the Captain, and to act upon it. Ten marks for the first to do so, nine for the second, and so on.

VII. Correct the following : " As the Guide
Corps swung sharply round the corner,
at a pace with which the juniors at
the rear could hardly keep up, they
nearly collided with the Divisional
Commissioner ; very smart with her
saxe-blue cords. The entire party
saluted smartly, and went on to the
wood where cowslips were reported
in full bloom. It was good to be
alive on such a perfect June day,
with the corn already turning golden,
and the air thrilling with the
cuckoo's liquid note. Nora, who
though only thirteen, wore already
the white stripe of a Patrol Leader,
and dozens of proficiency badges, in-
cluding the prized First Aid, upon her
left arm, shouted gaily : ' Come on !
I can see our wood is all bluebells
and cowslips. . . .' "

" Lor !—I mean, less vulgarly, my only
aunt ! The Captain has been busy," M. M.
murmured admiringly, as she skimmed this
effusion. " Now, Swallows, on to it ; we
mustn't waste a second, or let K. down !—
Peggy, you're pretty fair at signalling—will
you take the Morse message ? We're short

of time, but if each of the Swallows is responsible for something—Judy, you do the Nature stunt ; we're opposite Margaret, thanks be ! and she's quick in the uptake. . . . You new Tenderfoots, ever sewn on a linen button, Brenda ? "

" Never," Brenda said ; " but I think I could make it stay on, if that's what you mean."

" I don't. It's got to be sewn on the right way or we lose marks. Nancy, you !—look slippy ! "

Nancy was down in a corner in a moment, stitching for dear life.

" Who has the Electrician's Badge—Sanna, you—catch on to these wires and join them ; 'member what they told us to do when a wire fuses out in the country, and the nearest electrician is eight miles away. . . . We've only fourteen minutes. . . ."

" Can't I help ? " Brenda begged. She was conscious of a real keen desire that the Swallows should be the Patrol that came out top, and the Robins on their right seemed getting on horribly fast with the tests in their envelopes.

" Course you can—you shall—oh, I know —pack for the week-end. Run, Brenda, and for any sake, don't be late bringing the suit-

case down—you have thirteen minutes—
and don't forget your toothbrush ! "

Brenda ran. She did not say this time
that she had never packed a suit-case. She
wanted to work for the Patrol, and there
seemed to be enough for every one to do.

She landed in her bedroom, breathless,
and dragged out the suit-case from under-
neath her bed, and opened it. Then she was
faced with a horrible feeling of helplessness.
What did you take for the week-end ?

She had never packed for herself in all
her life ; she had never even seen it done,
or had any voice in what she took away
with her. She had occasionally paid visits
to relatives, but never for so short a time
as a week-end ; and there were the migrations
to Castle Helsingfoss. But the Lord Cham-
berlain informed Miss Heron, and Miss
Heron informed Annette, Brenda's French
maid, how long the visit was to be, and
whether any public appearances would be
included in it, and Brenda had nothing to
say in the matter. She would have given a
good deal for a word with Annette, just then.

But that was impossible, and precious
minutes were racing by. She opened a
drawer, snatched out three clean nightdresses
and swept the top of the chest of drawers

bare of her ivory and silver toilet set. It seemed to take up a great deal of room in the suit-case.

" A toothbrush ! " M. M. had impressed upon her—a rush to the wash-stand, and sponges, toothbrush, nail-brush, tubes of tooth-paste, and all were jammed together in a damp and knobbly bundle in her sponge-bag. Hurled in on the top of the night-dresses, it stuck up well beyond the top of the suit-case. Brenda looked at it despairingly for a moment, tried to flatten it into a more convenient shape, and finally took out the nail-brush and one tube of tooth-paste and threw them in loose.

There seemed to be extraordinarily little room in a suit-case, she thought, and it was difficult to remember everything with that horrible sense of hurry. Finally she put in an evening frock but no petticoat, bedroom slippers, but no indoor shoes, and four pairs of stockings. Annette always changed her stockings for her when she changed her dress. She had not a notion how to fold her evening frock, but believed tissue paper came somehow into the packing of it, and there was tissue paper in her hat-box. Brenda made a dash for it, saw by her watch that she had only two minutes longer, thrust in the evening frock — and then the suit-case would not shut.

Something must come out ; a desperate dive, and an ivory clothes-brush and flask of lavender water were cast all anyhow upon the floor, and Brenda knelt on the case and forced the clasps to. A breakneck rush downstairs, and she handed in her suit-case to Miss Ferrars, last of all the ten.

Miss Ferrars and Miss Kean unpacked each suit-case, and marked for a good choice and the way it was packed. Brenda's suit-case scored only six marks out of the twenty which were the maximum, and Brenda could not be altogether surprised, when she saw how many really important things she had forgotten, and how neatly the Robins and Nightingales had packed their two cases, making use of every available inch of space in the way they arranged everything. However, M. M. was extremely nice about it, when Brenda made her way to her in much compunction after the suit-cases had been criticised and marked.

" I expect I should have got about three marks myself," she said cheerfully. " *I* can't pack for nuts " ; and Brenda thought that a particularly nice way of putting her failure, for a person who had scored almost

the maximum in her correction of the bit
of Guide description, with its carefully prepared pitfalls, and with only five minutes
to do it in.

The writing and spelling were wild, but
Miss Ferrars had made no unkind allusions to
that fact; she praised the observation shown.

" You talk about a Guide *Company*, not
Corps," M. M. had written. " You never
have your juniors in the rear on a march;
they go in the middle. A Divisional Commissioner wears silver cords, saxe-blue are a
District Commissioner's. They wouldn't all
salute—just the senior Guider; she would
say, ' Eyes right,' or ' Eyes left,' and the
Guides would do it. Cowslips aren't so
much in woods as in fields and on downs—
anyhow, not in June. The cuckoo is getting
on the move in June, and his note isn't
specially liquid then. The corn isn't turning
yellow. A P.L. wears *two* white stripes on
her pocket. You wouldn't have shoals of
badges at thirteen, because you could only
have been a Guide for two years. The
First-Aid Badge is worn on the right sleeve,
because it is one of the badges that specially
helps other people, and a Guide wouldn't
be allowed to take it so young."

When the marks for every test in the

envelopes had been added for each Patrol,
the Swallows stood fourth out of ten—
Robins, Blackbirds, and Bantams coming
before them.

Katharine, surrounded by her Patrol as
soon as the Captain released her, thought
it " jolly good." Brenda determined inwardly that she would learn the way to pack
a suit-case before the next Guide meeting.

Several quick, short blasts from the
Captain's whistle brought the P.L.'s in a
circle round the Guiders, and their Patrols
fell in, in file, behind them, so as to radiate
outward in star formation. Brenda expected the " Dismiss ! " and was a good deal
surprised when, started by the Captain, all
the Company began to sing together. She
could not join in, naturally, knowing neither
words nor music : she listened instead.

She had heard the National Anthem of
Nystrea sung by massed thousands on her
father's birthday ; but it had hardly stirred
her as this did.

The words were set to a simple marching
tune—and every Guide was singing them :

" Marching, marching, marching ever forward !
   On to the portals, opened wide,
   Where enthroned are Loyalty and Service.
   Forward, forward, forward, every Guide ! "

CHAPTER VII

IN THE LUMBER-ROOM

M. M. had been very nice over that suit-case business, Brenda considered; and the immediate result of the Guide competition was to make her feel much more friendly towards M. M.

That was lucky, for on the Sunday morning Katharine woke up alarmingly hoarse; and M. M. promptly fetched Matron. It appeared that " throats " were a crime of Katharine's, and had to be looked after. Matron took her temperature, asked her whether she had been doing something silly, and ordered her into dressing-gown and slippers and to come to the San. wing for a day or two.

Brenda and M. M. were left to make the best they could of each other, and got on better than might have been expected. They walked to church together, and M. M. promised help with Brenda's " knots " tomorrow. On the way back M. M. asked about Nystrean services and whether the sermons were longer than in England, and Brenda described the usual Sunday of Carol and herself.

" Oh, you may play games then in the afternoon ; *we* mayn't," M. M. explained. " Lucky you mentioned it to me—there would have been wigs on the green if Miss Christopherson caught you inciting the Juniors to tennis on a Sunday afternoon. Still, our Sundays are all right ; go on about yours. What else do you do besides the very long service in the Cathedral or your private chapel, and a gay afternoon ? "

" Generally we lunch with my father," Brenda said.

" Oh ! all right, I should think," M. M. suggested tentatively.

" Well, it's a change from my everlasting schoolroom."

" I don't think I've ever seen a picture of King Conrad," M. M. remarked.

" Oh, he's very ordinary looking ; I'm afraid I didn't bring a photo, but I'll save the stamp on the next letter I have, if you like."

" I should be interested ; after all, a King is a King even if he doesn't look it," M. M. said kindly. " Haven't you got an old letter anywhere about, though ? "

" I'm sure I haven't; but—I know— Carol and I used to collect stamps a bit; and I believe Annette put the book in. If she did, we have all the Nystrean stamps from the beginning, and you can see Father at different ages. He began to reign when he was twenty-two."

" Oh, quite youngish."

" But he didn't look young; I don't believe he ever did."

" Sort of side-whiskers ? " M. M. wanted to know.

" Of course not ! " Brenda was rather offended. " He doesn't go back as long as that."

" Sorry; *I* didn't know," M. M. apologised. " I thought he sounded a bit stodgy, by what you say."

It was no good quarrelling with M. M., and Brenda was honest enough to acknowledge that it was her fault if M. M. had a rather unfavourable idea of King Conrad.

" He isn't exactly stodgy," she explained ; " only frightfully dull and particular about things, but I suppose he can't help that really; only it does make talking to your father a bit melancholy, if he is going to correct your grammar, and ask you if you haven't anything more sensible to say, and object to the things you've been doing, and be contemptuously surprised if you don't know all the horrible things in history and geography he asks you. . . ."

"Ghastly," M. M. sympathised. "My father hates us to be late for meals, and sometimes says my nails are an ' outrage,' but he isn't as bad as that."

"Oh, my father means to be kind, I think." Brenda again felt a qualm of compunction. "He has given me some lovely things—and he's really quite nice-looking, particularly in uniform."

"Didn't you unpack your stamp-book ? " M. M. asked.

"Matron put my things away—I'm sure I haven't seen it since I came. I haven't thought about it really."

"Let's look when we get in," suggested M. M., who always wanted to do things at once.

The walk from church was short of a mile, and they were at Beech House before half-past twelve. "Come along—loads of time," M. M. said cheerfully, and up the two went to their bedroom forthwith, and set to work with vigour to hunt in all Brenda's putting-away places, but without success. M. M. was very much annoyed.

" I do think you might have been interested enough to know where your own stamp-book was put," she complained. " Personally I consider it jolly distinguished to have a father whose head is on stamps."

It hadn't struck Brenda in that light, but she didn't want M. M. to find her stupid.

" There's a kind of pocket in my box; Annette might have put it there; it's a thin little book," she said. " If I knew where the boxes are kept. . . ."

" I can tell you; they're kept in the lumber-rooms at the top of the house. Beech House is pretty old, you know, and there are topping garrets. The maids used to sleep up there before Miss Christopherson's day, I believe; but she only uses them for our boxes. Wish she didn't; we could do all kinds of things there, if we could go up."

" What sort of things ? "

" Oh, telling ghost-stories and exploring and all that. There are some queer corners, as far as I remember, where you could imagine anything happening, and a place under the roof with no floor, no proper one, I mean."

" Why not go up ? " asked Brenda.

" I don't suppose it would matter, as you want your stamp-book," M. M. said.

" Come on, or we shall have the first gong
going."

They hurried upstairs, and came into the
first of the three long, low garrets which ran
nearly the whole length of the old part of
Beech House.

They *were* rather delightful and mysterious, Brenda thought, used as she was to
places that were always aggressively tidy
before she saw them. Even on this windy
sunny May morning, the Beech House
lumber-rooms were rather dark, because the
windows were small and low and heavily
gabled ; and there were, as M. M. had said,
queer and unexpected corners ; and the roof
came low, or rather the great beams that
crossed it—Margaret Reresby could hardly
have stood upright beneath some of these
—and sure enough, there was a space under
the roof which you got to by means of a
trap-door, where there was no floor, but
rough wooden planks laid edgeways, about
a foot apart, and plaster below. Boxes of
all shapes and sizes were piled and stacked
in the three lumber-rooms, but the two girls
didn't begin at once to look among them for
Brenda's. This place was more exciting
than any stamp-book.

" Couldn't we go in ? " Brenda asked,

her head and shoulders through the funny little trap-door in the wall, which was the entrance to this delightful spot.

" A bit dusty, I expect," M. M. thought, " still " — recklessly — " we've got clothes-brushes. Only don't put your feet between the planks, for any sake, or you'll go through somebody's ceiling, I guess."

" Rather a shock to any one below, if they saw a leg coming through," Brenda laughed, as she crawled cautiously through the trap-door, and landed her feet carefully on one of the planks crossing the floor.

" I should think it might be—let alone the fact that I expect we're not exactly sup-posed to be here at all," M. M. said, as she followed her.

It is to be feared that the last speech made the exploring more attractive, not less so to Princess Brenda. At home it was so very difficult to do anything that she ought not, with a governess or maid always with her ; there *was* an attraction about doing some-thing you were not supposed to do, just for once. She and M. M. explored that place under the roof with great thoroughness, stepping from plank to plank, and once nearly went through the ceiling below, when M. M. slipped and clung to Brenda for sup-

port ; and so came at last, in the very darkest
corner, where the roof came very low, to
that queer little hiding-hole under the tiles.

It is rather doubtful whether, even with
the thoroughness of their exploration, they
would have found it, for the place was distinctly dark, and the one small window
opaque with dirt, if it hadn't been in that
particular corner that M. M. missed her
footing on one of the planks, and only just
saved herself from the disaster of putting a
foot through the ceiling beneath, by a timely
clutch at Brenda. Brenda caught at the
wall to steady herself, and felt the little door,
tucked away between two joists.

" I say, do look at this ! " she cried.

" Look at what ? "

" I believe it's a door."

" What fun ! " cried M. M., and came to
her side to investigate.

It certainly seemed to be a little door, a
good deal smaller than the door they had
come through into the floorless room.

" I shouldn't wonder if it's an historic
hiding-hole," M. M. said, tugging at it with
a vigour that threatened to break her nails.
" Wonder if we shall make any thrilling
discoveries of Jacobite papers or that sort
of thing ? "

It didn't look as though they would make any discovery at all just then, for the door stuck like cobbler's wax. But just as a curiously faint far-away sound of a bell came to their ears, it gave quite suddenly, showing, as far as they could tell in the dim light, a tiny cupboard of a room, low-pitched and very dark.

But, thrilling though the discovery was, they had no time to enjoy it then.

" Come *on*! that was the lunch bell," M. M. gasped, seizing Brenda by the arm. " Hope to goodness it was the first—if not, we're done in. But there's only five minutes between them, anyway."

They got out of the floorless room as fast as they could, and that wasn't very fast, for it is extraordinarily difficult to be quick when you have to step from plank to plank on a narrow edge, and the light is more than bad. It had come on to rain while they were upstairs, and the whole place seemed in shadow. Still they got out, without putting a foot through between the planks, and in the stronger light of the lumber-room, looked at one another in some dismay.

Each saw a girl who was deplorably dusty and dirty ; luckily the day had looked so doubtful that the school had been told to put on their dark blue rep frocks instead of the white serge coats and skirts of a summer Sunday; even so they showed only too plainly in what sort of a place they had been.

" My word ! we must wash and brush up at the double ! " M. M. said.

Beech House allowed tidying to be done in bedrooms, but hands must be washed downstairs, in the Senior or Junior Dressing-Room, according to your place.

There was an ominous silence about the bedroom regions; no girls talking and laughing, or running along the passages on their way downstairs.

" Good gracious ! . It must have been the second bell we heard," groaned M. M. " I do hope it won't mean marks off for the House. Double-dyed asses we were not to leave the lumber-rooms alone till the afternoon ! "

They did a hasty and rather inadequate tidying, and fled to the dining-room. Yes, there was no doubt about it, they were late, horribly late; the hot roast beef or cold boiled chicken had all gone round; vegetables and salad handed; in some cases plates were half emptied already. Even Brenda saw the magnitude of the offence;

she had always been expected to be punctual at the Palace.

She walked up the long room to where Miss Christopherson sat at the head of the central table. "I must apologise, Miss Christopherson, but we really didn't hear the first gong," she explained, with dignity. "Of course I ought to have thought about the time, but I assure you my discourtesy was quite unintentional."

Brenda took her place, feeling comfortably sure that, if she had committed a rather serious offence, she had at least made full amends. Mariota, who had quite as much cause to apologise, only muttered, "I'm very sorry, Miss Christopherson."

It was never Miss Christopherson's way to scold on Sunday. She looked rather odd for a moment, Brenda thought; then she said, "Another time, listen for the gong; you should not be out of hearing at lunch-time," and then turned to Margaret and asked her how Colonel Reresby liked his new station? M. M. heaved a sigh of relief which was audible.

Nothing more was said then, but afterwards, in the Common Room, several girls from her own form surrounded Brenda and informed her kindly but firmly that

" cheeking Miss Christopherson " was " bad
form " and not done at Beech House ! It
took the puzzled Brenda several minutes to
discover that her apology was the " cheek "
referred to, and then in sheer self-defence
she had to explain that she really was out of
hearing, and give the reason.

Her crime was condoned, for the half-
dozen were wildly thrilled by the hiding-
hole under the eaves.

" What a place for a midnight supper ;
nobody would hear," suggested Rosemary
Cray.

CHAPTER VIII

PREPARATIONS

" MIDNIGHT suppers ! do you have them here ? " Brenda asked, surprised, for so far Beech House had been very unlike the schools of the few stories she had read.

" Sometimes ; but, worse luck ! they always have to be such horribly quiet affairs," Rosemary explained. " Miss Christopherson goes to bed frightfully late, and Matron sleeps with one ear open. . . . Let's have a look at this place of yours ! "

Brenda went willingly enough, relieved that Rosemary at least should have switched off from her unfortunate apology. M. M. was nowhere to be seen, but Brenda supposed that she wouldn't mind their joint discovery being shown without her.

She and Rosemary got the queer little narrow door open quite easily this time ; evidently it was only on occasions that it stuck ; and both crept inside, to find themselves in a tiny cupboard room with perhaps seven feet of depth and three of width, and a strong draught from somewhere between the tiles to the left, supplying air in the place of the window that was not there.

" A topping place, if we brought candles," Rosemary thought. " We should be right away from everybody."

Brenda agreed. " But it's awfully small."

" We needn't have many ; just a few who don't mind risking a row," said Rosemary, warming to it. " Thelma Wintoun, who sleeps with me, and Helen Quibly, and Pam Wildacre . . ."

" And M. M., of course ? She found the hole really," Brenda said.

" Yes, M. M., of course ; I think she'll be all right—and you and myself. . . . I should say six would be about as many as we could get in comfortably."

" Uncomfortably " would be nearer the mark, Brenda thought, looking at the sloping cupboard of a place ; but she was eager to taste the unknown delights of a midnight supper. At home she went to bed at a stated time, and stayed there. There was no object in getting up, because there was nobody to share in the adventure. Besides, it was rather pleasant to find herself so much

more popular than she had been hitherto—
Rosemary seemed to think it distinctly
brainy of M. M. and herself to have discovered so beautifully retired a spot for a
midnight supper.

" When shall we have it ? " she inquired,
making her way cautiously across the floor
of the unboarded room.

" It means a bit of planning first," Rosemary told her. " About the food and all
that."

" You mean what we have ? "

" No ; of course we shall settle that among
us—and it depends a bit how much money
we can raise ; I meant the getting hold of it."

" Can't we write an order and post it ? "

" You're new to school, aren't you ? "
Rosemary remarked. " Do you suppose
there wouldn't be questions asked, if parcels
of food addressed to us came arriving at
the back door ? Much midnight supper we
should get ! "

" I'll find a way," Brenda said con-
fidently. She liked her sudden popularity,
and had no intention of giving it up if she
could help it. It oughtn't to be difficult to
get enough food for six girls who had already
eaten four large meals that day, she thought.

And as a matter of fact it wasn't. For

Monday morning brought a letter for Miss
Christopherson, which made her look consideringly at Brenda, and detain her when
grace had been said, and the girls were preparing to leave the table.

"My dear, I have a letter from the
Nystrean Minister."

"Count Wrynder—oh, he and the Countess
promised they would come and look me up.
Vedelle is just my age, and used to come to
tea with me sometimes at home before they
came to England," Brenda said eagerly.

"Yes, dear, and I understand from the
Count that the King would be quite willing
for you to go out with the Count and
Countess, if it is according to our Beech
House rules. I don't generally allow my
girls to go out quite so early in the term, but
the Count writes that he is coming down to-
morrow to bring his boy to Motcombe House,
and he and the Countess would very much
like to be allowed to take you out to lunch.
You would like to go, I expect, and I am prepared to make an exception to my general
rule for this once."

"Oh, thank you!" Brenda said eagerly.

She had been under the impression before
she came to Beech House that she would be
glad to get as far away as possible from

every one to do with the old, dull Nystrean life, except, of course, for Carol ; but there was no denying that she felt quite pleased at the idea of meeting the Count and Countess again, and having a change from school. Of course they would ask Carol, too, and she would be able to find out how he was getting on at Rollincourt. None too well, she expected ; Carol was much shyer than herself.

Brenda remembered something as Miss Christopherson was turning away, with a kindly, " Then I will write to the Count at once and accept the invitation for you, Brenda."

" Miss Christopherson ? "

" Yes, Brenda."

" I am sorry that my apology for being late . . ."

Miss Christopherson smiled most forgivingly.

" Don't think anything more about it, my dear ; you are not used to the ways of school yet. I dare say that the other girls are excellent teachers for you—but probably rather plain spoken. I quite understand."

Brenda was glad that she had said it, though still she found it difficult to see where she had been to blame. However, that question didn't worry her long, for a delightful

thought had come into her head. Of course
this invitation made everything smooth for
the midnight supper. She could buy all that
she wanted when out with the Minister and
his wife.

She wanted to tell the good news to M. M.
or Rosemary at once ; but neither was to be
seen just then, and she was obliged to hurry
off to a music-room for the half-hour of
practice that must be got in before prayers
and morning school. As it was, it was a tight
fit to manage it, and she joined the stream of
girls pouring to the School Hall rather late,
and only came up with M. M. just at the
door.

" It's all right for the midnight supper,"
she whispered jubilantly.

M. M. did not look nearly so pleased and
excited as Brenda had expected.

" We couldn't do the food," she said, and
seemed more surprised than gratified by
Brenda's prompt answer, " *I* can ! "

Brenda could only suppose that she had
not liked the hiding-hole being shown without her, and yet, somehow, that didn't sound
like M. M. She was rather hurt by the
unsympathetic attitude, and then and there
decided to say nothing about the supper till
the food had been got. She had plenty of

money ; there was no need to ask for anybody's help.

She took out a school story from the
library, and, as she expected, found a full
description of a midnight feast. Her ideas
about food prices were of the vaguest, but
she put two pound notes into her bag when
she went to change her frock for going out
to lunch next day, and hoped for the best.

The Count and Countess were extremely
punctual, as befitted the representatives of
a country where the King was never for a
quarter of a minute late for anything.
Brenda had expected punctuality, and was
ready for the summons to the drawing-room.

The last few days had made such a difference that it felt almost odd to have the
Minister bending deferentially over her hand
as he took it, and asking whether this was a
convenient time for her to lunch. Brenda
went off with the Count and Countess very
cheerfully, and enjoyed her lunch at the
hotel. She only wished that Vedelle had
been there in the place of Eugene, whom she
had always found a shy and stupid little boy,
though Carol and he got on as well as could
be expected when one was ten and one was
twelve.

They were getting on very well now, for

Carol's few days at Rollincourt raised him
on a pinnacle in the eyes of a boy who was
going to school for the first time ; and it is
always agreeable to the new to find some
one who is newer. (By which it will be seen
that Brenda was right in guessing that she
would meet her brother at luncheon ; he
had been called for directly the Count,
Countess, and herself had left Beech House.)

During luncheon the point was raised—
what would the Prince and Princess like to
do during the hour after lunch before they
returned to their respective schools and the
Minister and his wife to town ? The Count
alone was taking his boy up to Motcombe
House, which stood a couple of miles away
from the hotel ; the Countess was quite at
the disposal of her guests.

" Oh, won't you come to my school with
me ? " Eugene begged of Carol ; " then you
could say if it's like yours. . . ."

Carol glanced rather nervously at Brenda,
but she was inclined to be gracious.

" I expect you could put Eugene in the
way of things," she said, " and, if the
Countess doesn't mind, I have a little
shopping to do, and should be quite busy
while you go up to Motcombe House."

So it was arranged, and Brenda attacked

her roast chicken with a comfortable sense
that things were working out most con-
veniently. The less people who knew about
a midnight supper, the better, and the
Countess would not be likely to ask incon-
venient questions.

They talked " schools " for nearly the
whole of lunch ; Carol seemed to be settling
down quite happily at Rollincourt. He
liked his form master, Nick Reresby, " the
one who caught you, Brenda," he explained,
Brenda thought unnecessarily ; everybody
talked of him as " Nick," Carol said, and
thought he knew it, though he pretended
that he didn't. Carol thought him " no
end of a chap." There were " awfully decent
chaps " in his room too, and he had hopes of
the Second Eleven. He and " two other
chaps " were to play in a test match next
week, and two of the three would be chosen.
Brenda realised with surprise that Carol
really seemed to be more of a success at
school than she was — or rather than she
had been ; this midnight feast was going to
make the other girls feel her a real sport,
and make her the popular heroine of a school
story.

She said good-bye to Eugene and hoped
he would like Motcombe House, and saw the

two boys drive away with Count Wrynder
in the car ; then she and the Countess went
on foot into the town.

" You are sure you don't mind walking ? "
asked the Countess.

" Rather not," Brenda said cordially ;
" but we may need a taxi back to the hotel.
I shall have a lot of parcels."

The Countess laughed. " That's easily
managed, but I can't think how you come
to want so much after less than a week at
school."

" I have a little party for some of the
girls," Brenda explained, quite under the
impression that she was really stating the
case, and not realising that the Countess took
it for an ordinary tea-party, authorised by
Miss Christopherson.

They got doughnuts, meringues, chocolate
éclairs, jam tartlets, and rich almond cake at
the confectioner's, a tin of sardines and of
biscuits, also bottles of fizzy lemonade at
the grocer's, and Brenda was right about
the parcels. Taken as provision for six
girls between supper and breakfast, they
seemed bulky.

" Don't you think you had better have
them sent round to Beech House direct ? "
suggested the Countess, rather doubtfully ;

but Brenda shook her head. She remembered Rosemary's comment.

" No, thanks; I would rather take them myself."

She took them back to the hotel in a taxi, and the hotel produced a large cardboard box, and packed them neatly for her, before the return of the Count and Carol in the car. There was only time for about five minutes' chat in the verandah outside the hotel, and then Brenda remarked that it was nearly three o'clock, and she and Carol must go.

The car was at Beech House in a minute or two. Brenda shook hands with the Count and Countess and said how much she had enjoyed herself, called a good-bye to Carol, and the Count lifted out the box and held it for her.

" Thanks so much," Brenda said, taking it from him.

" Jumpers ? " inquired Carol, with masculine scorn.

" Rather not ! " Brenda laughed, and took the box from the Count in a hurry, and opened the front door.

It was not quite three o'clock yet. Brenda ran up to her room, pushed the box out of sight under her bed, and scribbled a note to Rosemary :

" All ready for the supper to-night. Invite the others.—BRENDA."

As she passed Rosemary's desk on her way to her own, she dropped the little note on to her exercise-book, and was rewarded at tea-time by an approving whisper from Rosemary of " Sport ! "

CHAPTER IX

BRENDA'S FEAST

THE provisions were displayed to Rosemary and her room-mate, Thelma, and of course M. M. too, when the girls were supposed to be dressing for supper. Rosemary and Thelma were enthusiastic about quality and quantity, but M. M. seemed a little half-hearted. " There'll be no end of a row if we're caught," she muttered.

" That's the whole beauty of this place," Rosemary told her, exasperated. " We shan't be caught. Nobody could hear us if we shouted. What on earth's come over you, M. M. ? You never used to be afraid of a row ! "

" I'm not afraid ! " M. M. fired. " It isn't that."

" You're not going to get out of it at this eleventh hour ? " Brenda asked, rather dismayed. " You can't, when we found the place together ! "

" K. is a bit easy to rattle, I know, but *you* never were," Rosemary chimed in; and

Thelma added : " Oh, you must join in,
M. M. It wouldn't be half the fun without
you. Besides, it isn't fair to Brenda when
she's got this scrumptious spread."

" Oh, all right ; I'll come, then. Anything
for a quiet life," Mariota agreed ; and the
conspirators made hasty plans. Rosemary,
who could always stay awake when she
pleased, was to come along and wake
Brenda and M. M., when quite sure that Miss
Christopherson was safe in bed. Thelma
would wake the other pair meantime, and
then the six would tiptoe in procession to
the lumber-room, and begin to enjoy themselves.

" What about lights ? " M. M. asked.

" Isn't there electric light ? " Brenda
wanted to know.

" Not in the garrets ; it's an old house,
you know, and it wasn't installed when
Miss Christopherson came. She didn't
bother to put it in the lumber-rooms,"
M. M. explained.

" Well, I've a torch," Rosemary said. " I
think it wasn't damaged much when it
rolled off the chest of drawers last week.
Besides, we can take candles."

At Beech House the bedroom switches
were outside the rooms, and every bedroom

was provided with a candlestick and matches
in case a girl should feel ill and want somebody to go in search of Matron.

" Oh yes, we can take our candles, but
there won't be much room for them in our
hiding-hole," M. M. thought. " We'll hope
your torch is all right, Rosemary."

" I doubt its lasting through the gorgeous
spread Brenda has provided," Rosemary
said handsomely, and Brenda felt gratified.
It was pleasant to be popular ! She didn't
worry about the lighting problem.

There was a great scramble to dress for
supper, and the second bell went before any
of the conspirators were really ready. But
present-day frocks require no fastening, and
if hair was rather wild there was always the
chance that among so many girls it would
not be noticed. Brenda and M. M. dashed
down together and got in at the tail-end of
the long procession pouring in at the door of
the dining-room.

Six girls dealt delicately with fishcakes,
blancmange, and stewed rhubarb, in view
of the feast to come. Miss Christopherson
happened to notice Brenda.

" You don't seem hungry to-night, my
dear ; how is that ? "

" Brenda went out to lunch, Miss Christopherson," suggested M. M. with a grin, and Miss Christopherson laughed.

" Is that the result of personal experience, Mariota ? "

No further question was asked.

Bedtime was unusually long in coming to six Beech House girls ; but it came at last ; and Brenda and Mariota were free to talk.

" I've always wondered what this sort of thing would be like," Brenda said.

" Oh, it's great sport," M. M. allowed. " Haven't you ever . . . ? "

" No."

" Oh, well, I hope you'll enjoy it.   I think you ought to see what it's like—for once, anyhow."

" I shan't stop at doing it once, if a midnight supper is half the fun that books make out," Brenda assured her.   " I've got some arrears of fun to make up, by now."

M. M. seemed sorry for her.   " If you don't mind my asking, do you have to do public appearances and opening wings of hospitals all your time ? " she inquired.

Brenda groaned tragically.   " Oh no ; I shouldn't mind that half so much.   I'm generally at lessons.   Carol, my brother, does all the interesting things."

" What a shame ! " M. M. sympathised.
" Anyway, you're doing something to-night.
I wonder ? "

" You wonder what ? "

M. M., now in her dressing-gown, laughed
and opened the door a cautious chink to
peer out.

" I wonder whether I could possibly get
along to Judy's room without being spotted ?
I know she has a torch."

" Did you mean to borrow it ?   But then,
Judy would want to come, wouldn't she ?
and there simply won't be room."

" She won't ! " M. M. was indignant.
" Judy won't ask any question ; she isn't
that sort.   Besides, it isn't my party."

" We couldn't borrow her torch and not
ask her, surely ? " Brenda thought.   " Do
you want that torch so very particularly ? "

" Well, if Rosemary's should give out."

" We've got candles."

" None too safe ; remember the draughts."

" Oh, well, ask Judy then, only ask her
to join us as well," Brenda said impatiently.

M. M. hesitated.   " Really, I don't think
we ought ; thanks, Brenda.   We should be
jammed like sardines—the fit will be tight
for six."

They had left it too late ; the silence bell

rang out, and Beech House said its prayers, to a more or less degree.

Ten minutes after silence bell would come " Lights "; it was clearly impossible to get to a bedroom, the length of two passages away, in the little interval that would remain after prayers were said. It would probably mean walking straight into the arms of the mistress taking " Lights," and being expected to explain why you were breaking rules by being out of your room at this time of the evening. Brenda's week at school had enlightened her to that extent, and she was relieved when Mariota said, in a low voice, " I couldn't do it in the time, so it settles itself that way."

The two got into bed. " I hope you don't mind ? " Brenda said politely.

" No—o ! As long as Rosemary's torch is all right," M. M. said; and then " Lights " were taken, and Miss Crayshaw's footsteps died away down the passage, and silence reigned. Officially the Beech House girls were asleep. Actually, Brenda and M. M. at least were not.

Brenda was far too much excited for sleep, and kept on starting up, thinking that she heard Rosemary's tap at the door; and M. M., though quieter, was awake enough to say, " Don't be so silly," in tones that verged on the cross.

Nine had struck just before " Lights " were taken. Brenda heard the ten strokes booming out, and then eleven. The Staff had long since gone to bed ; Miss Christopherson must have gone too, surely ?

" M. M. ! " she whispered cautiously, " are you asleep ? "

" Getting a bit near it," M. M. whispered back.

" Do stay awake ! it must be almost time. Do you think Rosemary's forgotten ? "

" Not she ! "

" Shall we get up without waiting for her ? "

" If you want Miss Christopherson walking in and wanting to know who's ill and needing Matron," M. M. suggested.

Brenda lay down again pretty quickly ; whatever else she might want, it wasn't that. A very long quarter of an hour went by, and, to her disgust, she found herself getting, like M. M., a little too near the sleepy stage, now that the long waiting-time was so nearly over.

That would never do : she sat up determinedly, and felt for her dressing-gown.

" I'm not going to wait any longer for anybody ; of course Miss Christopherson has

gone to bed by now, and probably Rosemary
is asleep. Do go and wake her and Thelma,
while I get out the box."

M. M. groaned and rolled over.

" Ugh ! I was just dreaming it was all
over and I'd eaten six meringues. . . . What
do you want done ? "

" Well, we don't want to wait till morning,
do we, to begin our supper ? " Brenda suggested briskly, and M. M. got out of bed
obediently. " Anything for a quiet life ! "
she murmured as usual.

She slid out quietly into the passage.

" Hope I shan't walk bang into Miss
Christopherson ! "

She disappeared. Brenda lit her candle
and got out the box, so as to waste no time
when M. M. had roused up the rest.

She did not feel sleepy any longer now,
only thrilled and excited. Hitherto perhaps
school had hardly come up to her expecta-
tions, but this was the real thing at last !

It seemed a long time before M. M. came
back ; as a matter of fact it *was* rather a long
time, for she had found Rosemary and
Thelma distinctly hard to convince that it
was safe to begin proceedings at only twenty
past eleven, when Miss Christopherson was
known to be a person who sat up late.   How-

ever, she had brought them, and now that they were up, they were all prepared to enjoy themselves, and in so hilarious a mood that giggles were hard to repress.

The ghostly procession in dressing-gowns, M. M. and Brenda leading, crept on elaborate tiptoe along passages and up stairs, with queer little choked noises breaking from one or another, and rather doing away with the effect of the tiptoe; and arrived in the lumber-rooms at last.

They looked dark, limitless, and somewhat eerie in the faint light of Rosemary's torch. Pam Wildacre stumbled into a pile of suit-cases, and knocked the top one down with a thud that brought everybody's heart into her mouth. What if they should have been heard ?

But Miss Christopherson herself slept on the first floor, it was a comfort to remember ; it wasn't likely she would hear a tumbling suit-case through two floors. After about a minute and a half of breathless listening, several people told Pam what they thought of her, and Helen lit her candle.

" Just for getting us through the lumber-rooms," she said ; " we don't want Pam or anybody to overturn another lot."

" We never got your stamp-case after all,

when we were here on Sunday," M. M. said regretfully to Brenda.

" No more we did, but we can't stop to hunt now," Brenda told her. She was much more interested in the supper than in the stamps of her native country.

The candle flickered in the draughts, but it was a great comfort, and by its light the six girls and the cardboard box of provisions got safely across the boardless floor and into the hiding-hole. It was a very tight fit, but they *did* get in.

" Put the candle out," M. M. said rather anxiously to Helen.

The sloping roof came low above their heads, as the six crouched there ; the candle guttered wildly, for it was more draughty in this confined space than it had been in the big old rooms through which they had been passing.

" No, shut the door," Rosemary ordered. " It's the open door makes it so draughty, and we must have light for putting out the food. Shut it, Pam."

Brenda, on her knees beside her box, looked up to say impatiently, " Yes, shut it, or we'll have the candle over."

" Use Rosemary's torch," urged M. M.

But Rosemary's torch, which had been

decidedly dim in the first lumber-room, now
seemed inclined to strike work altogether.

" We can't put out the food in the dark,"
Brenda declared, and Pam slammed the little
door to, with some force.

Now that the door was shut, the hiding-
hole appeared extraordinarily small.   There
didn't seem to be room for anybody's legs,
and it was very difficult for Brenda to put
the food out without driving her elbows into
one or another of her guests.

" Do you know, I think we shall have to
help ourselves from the box," she said at
last.   " If I balance the candle on the corner
of it—like this—every one can see what there
is and help themselves.   I'll clear off some
of the papers."

She tossed down half a dozen sticky bags
beside the box, and dropped back meringues,
doughnuts, and éclairs on the top of the
other cakes.

" Come on, help yourselves," she said.
" Don't mind digging down into the box for
what you want."

Everybody laughed, and there was a
general scrimmage, as five girls accepted her
invitation at the same moment.   Luckily she
still had a steadying hand on the candle.
M. M. stood up, or at least as nearly stood

as the lowness of the roof allowed, holding a meringue in one hand and a doughnut in the other. She was greeted with laughter and cheers.

" Good old M. M. ! "

" Go it, M. M. ! "

" Give us a speech, M. M. ! "

" That's what I mean to do, as soon as you've all done interrupting," M. M. said. " I'm going to propose the health of Princess Brenda of Nystrea. She's given us a topping spread and been a real sport about it." (" Hear ! Hear ! ") " In compliment to her, I propose to search her suit-case—if, as I think, it was on the pile barged into by Pam —for the book containing the stamps of her native land. . . ." (" Tell us something else ! . . . M. M. leave a spread like this to go and find anything ! ")

" I didn't say *when* the search was to take place," M. M. concluded, undisturbed. " I merely said it would. My anxiety to behold the lineaments of King Conrad can wait till meringues have ceased to melt in my mouth and even éclairs cloy ; but it is there, the genuine anxiety. Brenda, all luck to Nystrea, and your very good health ! "

Brenda, laughing more than she had ever

done in her life before, tried to stand up
and bow her acknowledgments. One foot
had gone to sleep, in her cramped position,
and she waggled, catching at Rosemary's
shoulder. Rosemary's elbow came into
contact with the corner of the box—and—
nobody knew how it was exactly—but there
was a sharp cry from Pam. The candle
had swayed and toppled over all alight, upon
the sticky paper bags.

A flame shot up: four cramped and
tightly wedged girls tried to scramble to
their feet. Rosemary shrieked, " Open the
door, M. M. ! "

M. M. shook it—banged—pushed with all
her frightened strength. It wouldn't budge;
it had stuck !

CHAPTER X

RETRIBUTION

BRENDA suddenly realised the appalling danger into which her feast had brought five other girls.

The flames were shooting up horribly; the box was burning now, as well as the loose papers, the sugar on so many of the cakes adding fearful aliment to the fire. And they were trapped in a hiding-hole little bigger than a cupboard; already they could feel the scorch of the flames, and Mariota's frantic efforts to open the door seemed unavailing. It had stuck again as it had stuck before, only much tighter. Brenda remembered how Pam Wildacre had banged it; that had probably done the mischief. And the draughts were blowing the flames this way and that; the girls, shrunk back into the farthest corners of their hiding-hole as they were now, could not escape them long. Of course somebody ought to have crushed a dressing-gown and all her weight upon the paper when it first caught; but it all happened so horribly fast, that one didn't really know till it was too late.

None of M. M.'s instructions for the Fire-Brigade Badge covered this emergency, but Brenda made a desperate dash from her corner and sprang at the stuck door; feeling a tongue of flame dart at her as she did so, for the burning box was horribly near. But she couldn't leave M. M. to face the job all alone, and the double weight at the door might burst it open.

Together they pushed and shook ; a run back to get force to throw their weight upon the door was out of the question, of course, on account of the burning box ; but they put every ounce of strength they had into the struggle to free four and themselves.

It seemed an endless ghastly nightmare—really the whole thing probably was over in about a minute. Just as Helen screamed out "You're on fire, M. M. ! " somebody spoke outside. "Keep back, girls ! " and something heavy struck the jammed door sideways.

It flew open. M. M., who could not keep back, because there was no space to move, tumbled out head first, and was promptly enveloped in the heavy fur coat that Miss Christopherson wore over her evening dress, and the smoulder of fire extinguished.

The rest were out in a second; scorched, half-choked, and terribly scared, but un-damaged.

Miss Christopherson drew away her cloak from Mariota, carefully; and then shut to the door of the hiding-hole that had so nearly proved a death-trap.

Far from shutting too firmly, as before, the door, since the bang with a suit-case which had released it, refused now to close at all. Using her cloak for protection, for the wood was growing hot, Miss Christopher-son stood against the door and held it close, shutting in the flames for the time being.

"Take my candle, girls—carefully over this floor, please," she directed, as quietly as though this sort of thing was part of the ordinary school curriculum. "One of you phone over to Comber's cottage and send him here."

"May we bring up the fire-extinguishers, please?" M. M. asked imploringly. "Miss Christopherson, do let us help somehow!"

"Very well; don't make a noise and wake everybody," Miss Christopherson said, and the girls hurried as well as they could, con-sidering the trembling of their knees.

There was no time for thinking of conse-quences; all the six realised that the fire must be got under before it took a hold on the roof. Rosemary dashed for the telephone, which had a private line through to the chauffeur's cottage; and the others each seized one of the newest things in fire-extinguishers, and rushed upstairs to the garrets again.

The fire was out before Comber could get over, and, though a beam in the roof was smouldering, little real damage had been done.

By this time Matron, Miss Kean, Margaret Reresby, and two or three of the maids had been roused by the disturbance, and Miss Christopherson was more anxious to avoid waking other people than to look into the cause of everything just then.

" Everybody is to go quietly back to bed at once, please," she said, with authority. " Matron, would you kindly see if Mariota is hurt; her dressing-gown had caught. No one is to talk when once in bed. I shall see you six to-morrow morning after breakfast. You may consider yourselves very lucky that I had not gone to bed, and heard you in the garrets."

" Yes, Miss Christopherson. Thank you," M. M. answered dejectedly for the rest, and she and Brenda were hustled to their room by Matron.

M. M. proved to have a slight scorch on one leg; Matron went for lint and carron oil, and Brenda had the chance of asking questions.

" I don't think Miss Christopherson is so frightfully angry, do you ? "

" You don't know Miss Christopherson," M. M. said gloomily.   Her leg smarted.

" They say a great deal more to me at home for very much less, I can tell you," Brenda persisted.

" We still have to hear what Miss Christopherson says," M. M. reminded her.

" Well, of course, I shall let her know it was my affair."   Brenda was lofty.

" A fat lot of good that will do."   M. M. would not be comforted.   " She will say we knew it was a mug's game to go and shut ourselves into a place like that—it was, of course—and we knew the rules.   No, we're for it with our Miss Christopherson, I'm afraid ; and four of us B. House, too ! "

Matron came back, brisk and bracing and not at all sympathetic.   The dressing of the scorched leg was done to an accompaniment of true but tedious statements to the effect that M. M. had only herself to thank for it, and that all the girls had behaved idiotically, more like babies in the First Form than great girls in IVB, and they might be very thankful they had got off as lightly as they had. It was really rather a comfort when Matron had finished and put out the light, even though the two were left to the depressing reflection that they were in for a really first-class row, without the consolation that they had enjoyed themselves first. There had hardly been time for one éclair before the candle went over.

Brenda lay awake for some time after Mariota had dropped asleep, thinking over what she meant to say to Miss Christopherson to-morrow. She would be magnanimous and take the entire blame upon herself, though it had been Rosemary who suggested the hiding-hole for a midnight supper. Still she, Brenda, *had* bought the food, and it should be easy enough to help herself to a little more of the blame than really belonged to her share. The speech that Brenda composed as she lay in bed relegated the other five entirely to the ranks of the led : Brenda couldn't help feeling rather pleased with it. In a flash she saw herself toiling at a punish-ment-lesson of terrific length while the others enjoyed themselves at the tennis courts, free and happy because she had been generous in her confession. M. M. had been gloomy to-night, but then her leg was hurting, and she did not know how splendidly Brenda meant to behave when sent for to Miss Christopherson to-morrow. " She's a real sport," she heard the others say, and went to sleep at last, feeling almost happy in spite of the failure of the midnight feast. It would be something like her dreams if she could be " a sport " in the eyes of Beech House !

.   .   .   .   .   .

The summons to Miss Christopherson's room came, as expected, directly after breakfast, to the guilty six. On the way there Brenda, marching jauntily in front, turned round to say firmly to the rest : " You leave it all to me ; this is my affair."

The reception of that speech was not encouraging. Rosemary said, " What on earth are you talking about ? " and M. M., " Don't be an ass ! "

Brenda subsided for the moment. Let them wait ; they would soon see ! Borne up by the consciousness of her heroic intentions, she was quite cheerful and at ease when she came into Miss Christopherson's room, in conspicuous contrast to the other five.

" Good morning, Miss Christopherson ; I want to say at once——" she was beginning brightly, when Miss Christopherson interrupted, and in a most annihilating voice, though she did not raise it :

" Stand there, girls ! " She pointed to the centre of the room, and the dejected huddle by the door were obliged to come forward.

Brenda was easily first at the appointed spot, and began again : " I want to say at once that——"

" Kindly wait to answer my questions, Brenda," Miss Christopherson told her, and this time Brenda did realise the snub. " You all know that midnight suppers are against my rules ? "

" Yes, Miss Christopherson." An extraordinarily small volume of sound to come from five good-sized girls with healthy lungs. Brenda did not even trouble to answer that question ; she was waiting her chance to be generous and self-sacrificing on a large scale.

" And that you are not supposed to be in the garrets, except when you take up or fetch your suit-cases ? "

" Yes, Miss Christopherson."

" Who got the food for this feast—for you had food, I suppose ? "

" There wasn't time to have much before it was on fire," M. M. mumbled ruefully.

" A very good thing," Miss Christopherson said, most unsympathetically. " How did you buy what you had ? "

Brenda's chance at last ! She stepped forward. " If you will let the others go, Miss Christopherson, I shall be glad to tell you all about it," she said. " *I* was entirely responsible ; I got the cakes and things when I went out to luncheon yesterday, and then . . ."

" That will do, Brenda. You bought the food ? "

" And was responsible for . . ."

" I want answers to my questions and no other conversation, please, at present. How much did you spend ? "

" Really, I don't quite know, but . . ."

" Find out before this evening, and give in any money you may have remaining to Miss Kean. Was this shopping done with the knowledge of Countess Wrynder ? "

" Yes. Well, not exactly. I don't think she knew quite . . ."

" I hope not. But you took a most unjustifiable advantage of being allowed to go out with people who were strangers to our school rules, Brenda. When you come to think things over, you will see, I think, that what you did was not exactly honour-

able. No, don't speak now! I intend to
do the speaking. . . . You are six girls who
are all about fourteen and should have a
reasonable amount of sense. Midnight
suppers are not a great crime in themselves,
but you know perfectly well that they are
forbidden in this school, because several
silly girls have caught serious colds that
way and made themselves ill by eating rich
and indigestible things in the middle of the
night. Rules are not made without reason ;
you should be old enough to see that for
yourselves. To avoid the risk of being
discovered breaking rules, you girls from
IVв did something so desperately silly that
I should hardly have expected it from the
kindergarten class."

" I know it was idiotic about the candle,"
M. M. confessed. She made no effort to
justify herself, or to say that she had at
least protested against the use of a candle.
" I'd forgotten that the door was inclined to
stick, Miss Christopherson."

" Then you had been there before ? "

Brenda found her tongue again :

" As I tried to tell you before, Miss
Christopherson, I alone am really to blame
for this business. I wanted to explore when
we were looking for something I had left in

my suit-case, and found the hiding-hole;
and then I told the others——"

"I found the hole, just as much as you
did," M. M. said, rather crossly. "Miss
Christopherson, I know we've behaved
awfully stupidly, but . . . but, it wasn't
all fixed up—it just happened, except going
up to find Brenda's stamp-book, and that
was my idea."

"It wasn't one more than another, Miss
Christopherson," Pam volunteered. "We
were all in the supper business."

"So I supposed."

"But, Miss Christopherson, I assure
you——" poor Brenda began again wildly,
but Miss Christopherson held up her hand.

"That is enough, Brenda! You have all
behaved in a way of which I had thought
girls of your age quite incapable, and it is
only by the greatest good fortune that the
consequences have not been too horrible to
bear thinking of. The garrets are absolutely forbidden for the future to all the
school except the Sixth. You girls will
each take a conduct mark, and have all
the privileges of the Upper School sus-
pended for a week from to-day. That is
all; but take care how I have to speak to
any of you about breaking rules again!"

The six sinners filed out, most dejectedly.

" My word ! " groaned M. M. outside. " Twenty marks off B. House.   Help ! "

" If I had been allowed to explain . . ." Brenda began hotly.

M. M. took her arm, and impelled her firmly in the direction of IVʙ classroom.

" You mean all right, Brenda," she said, " but do try and believe you're not everybody.   We'd like you better that way."

CHAPTER XI

THE PHILANTHROPIST

ONE of the privileges of the Upper School withdrawn from the erring six was the use of the Senior Common Room. Now for a whole week they would have to share the Junior Playroom with some twenty-five " kids " ranging in age from seven to thirteen.

" Sickening ! " said Rosemary. " I do hope it's fine all the week, so we needn't go in."

But the second day after the fiasco of the midnight feast was cold and windy, with fierce scudding showers, and a good deal of time had to be spent indoors.

" Let's get a quiet corner to ourselves and read," suggested Helen Quigly. " Those little blighters will be absolutely beyond themselves if we take any notice of them."

" Let's try it, and see what happens," Brenda suggested lazily. She had always felt rather inclined to see something more of Pris and Penny, only Mariota had been so discouraging. But here was a chance thrown directly in her way; it was, of course, absurd to sit loftily apart all the time that they were forced to share the Juniors' play-room.

"You'll see fast enough," Rosemary told her gloomily.

"I like experiments," was Brenda's answer, and she strolled over to a noisy group of Juniors, among whom she had recognised the two small, fair bobbed heads and impish faces.

"Hullo, you two!" she said affably. "What are you playing at?"

Pris and Penny looked at one another doubtfully, and a rather aggressive-looking child of twelve pushed forward.

"Look here, we don't see why you should come and boss us, and laugh, just because you're Upper School and think you're doing us a favour by talking to us. This is *our* playroom."

Brenda laughed. "Of course it is; and I promise you I didn't mean to boss, what-ever that may be: I suppose it's something disagreeable? I just wanted to know about the doings of these two—because I knew them in Nystrea."

"Oh, that's all right," the aggressive

child, whom Brenda believed she had heard addressed as Molly Knight, informed her, much more affably ; and Pris and Penny were ready enough to make her free of the game. Brenda played vigorously with the Juniors till tea-time, ignoring the rather contemptuous expression on the faces of her own contemporaries, and was implored to " play with us again " by at least twelve out of the twenty-five at the tops of their voices when the tea bell rang.

For three days she spent a good deal of her spare time with the First and Second Forms, finding their whole-hearted admiration very soothing after M.. M.'s bracing attitude. And so came the Saturday when things happened.

It was a lovely day and a half-holiday, and the school was spending it on the beach. The Sixth, Fifth, Upper and Lower, and IVA and IVB, had been allowed to bathe, but, of course, the guilty six were out of it this week, and looked on enviously.

" Wish to goodness nobody had ever thought of that silly supper ! " groaned Pam. It was probably just a general complaint at their hard fate, and not in any way intended for an attack on Brenda ; but Brenda felt annoyed by the ingratitude. After all, one pound three and sixpence of her money had been wasted over that fiasco of a supper, and *she* wasn't grumbling. She got up, and walked away from her companions in misfortune, without another word.

" What's up ? " she heard M. M. ask lazily, and Pam's answer was quite painfully distinct:

" Oh, only Brenda, ratty about nothing, as usual."

With her head held high, Brenda strolled to the next cove, where she knew that she would find the junior forms making sandcastles. Paddling had been refused to Forms I. and II. because there were some colds among them.

The Juniors sighted Brenda as soon as she came round into the cove, and rushed to meet her with shrieks of joy. Miss Hunt, the mistress in charge, just looked up to see what the shrieks meant, and then went on placidly with her book. The sands were perfectly safe and the tide was low ; there was nothing needing her attention in the fact that a IVв girl had come to play with the babies.

" Come and tell us some more about Nystrea," begged Penny. " I'm tired of playing, and awfully hot."

"Isn't it a shame we mayn't paddle?"
Pris said. "I don't believe I'll ever be cool
again!"

"I know what I'd like," Betty Relton
mentioned, snuggling affectionately up to
Brenda as she sat down on the sand. "I'd
love an ice—a big strawberry one."

"Oh, so would *I*!" Penny burst in.
"Playing on the sands does make you hot
when you mayn't paddle."

Brenda had money on her, as it happened;
she had asked that morning for twenty-five
shillings out, to buy a Brownie camera for
Carol, whose twelfth birthday was on
Monday. But there would be plenty of
time to get the camera after tea.

"Well, if you want ices, you can have
them, I dare say," she said. "How many
are thirsty?"

All the children in hearing appeared to be
taken with a violent thirst at once.

"Twelve, thirteen, fourteen of you,"
Brenda counted. "There's a confectioner's
only just across the Parade, and we've got
nearly an hour still to tea-time."

The steps up to the Parade were only in
the next little cove: the children were half-
way up them before Brenda remembered
that she had said nothing to Miss Hunt.

That wasn't polite ; she might miss the children and wonder what had happened. But there wasn't time to go back all the way, or the children would be straggling across the Parade, without keeping a look out for passing cars. Brenda called from the side of the cove, so as not to waste time, " Just off for an ice ; back in half an hour," and dashed up the cliff steps after the children, without waiting in her haste to see if Miss Hunt had really heard.

The confectioner's she had noticed almost faced the steps on the opposite side of the Parade. It wasn't an extraordinarily high-class place, Brenda thought when she came to look at it closely ; but there wasn't time for hunting up a better, and the Juniors were not in the least inclined to be critical. She marched them in and seated them round two tables, the only two vacant, as it happened, for the shop was very full on this hot spring afternoon. Other people besides the Juniors of Beech House had evidently felt the need of ices.

The waitresses seemed to have more on their hands than they could manage ; the two girls, in limp mob caps and rather dirty flowered frocks, who were supposed to supply an eighteenth - century appearance to the

restaurant part of the confectioner's, were
flying about, trying to deal with the orders
of their numerous customers, and replying to
impatient grumbles with " Directly, Moddam.
Shan't keep you a minute, sir.   A little short-
'anded, Moddam."

It was hardly wonderful that Brenda found
her impatient signals were disregarded : the
harassed waitresses had heavy arrears of
orders to supply, and probably experience of
the many changes of mind that made the
taking of an order for school Juniors a very
lengthy affair.

Brenda wasn't used to being kept waiting,
and besides she had told Miss Hunt they
would only be gone half an hour, and she
had been trained to punctuality.   The tables
in the window were insufferably hot ; the
shop was airless, for the windows were all
tightly closed, presumably in a not altogether
successful attempt to keep out the flies, too
many of which were already buzzing about
the cakes and limp pastry displayed.

Brenda waited for some seven or eight
minutes, and through four repetitions of " In
a minute, Moddam."   Then she took action.
She wasn't at all used to waiting ; in
Nystrea, if she and her governess did go into
a shop of any kind, people stopped doing

other things and showed a flattering desire
that she should give an order. This kind of
attitude was unexpected and unpleasing.

She marched into the back part of the
shop, and accosted a worried waitress with a
dignity and decision which she probably found
startling.

" I am afraid I find it quite impossible to
wait any longer. Of course I see that you
are busy, but, if you cannot send anybody to
serve my party, I must take them elsewhere."

The waitress dropped the " Moddam " in
her surprise. " I'm sorry, Miss, I'm sure ;
but we're that busy and short-'anded . . .
I'll take your order."

" Thanks, and please send somebody along
with it really quickly, or the children won't
have time for their ices," Brenda requested.
" Surely you have other waitresses, in the
kitchen department, if not here ? "

The waitress looked helplessly at the other,
who had come up to see what all the trouble
was about, and something doubtful passed
about a certain " Florrie." Then Brenda's
waitress hurled a despairing " Directly,
Moddam," at three tables, and took Brenda's
order for " fourteen strawberry ices and
plenty of cakes, and send some one with them
at once, please, to the window tables."

A slovenly-looking girl appeared a minute
or two later, with a laden tray : Brenda was
too glad to see the ices appearing to trouble
much about the look of the attendant. The
eighteenth-century appearance was decidedly
missing in Florrie ; she wore a dirty pink silk
jumper, which had once belonged to somebody much bigger ; a navy pleated skirt a
little above her knees, and a not over-clean
apron, decidedly longer. Her age might
have been anything from fourteen to
eighteen, and she appeared to be suffering
from a very bad cold.

"That's right — put the saucers down
quickly," Brenda directed, " and then get
the bill for me, will you ?   I'll settle it while
we are having our cakes and ices, as we
haven't too much time. Never mind about
putting all the plates round ; we can pass
them ourselves."

Florrie withdrew, sniffing.

" She looks as though some one had been
pitching into her," remarked Penny the
experienced—" eyes all runny."

" *I* shouldn't mind *how* much I got pitched
into, if I lived in a place like this, where
I could have ices and cakes all day, if I
wanted," Pris chimed in ; and Brenda
laughed.

" I don't suppose she can ; probably she
has to go on ladling out ices for other people
all day, without thinking of getting even a
taste for herself."

" What a shame ! " Penny cried.   " Shall
I spoon a bit of mine on to the cake-plate,
Brenda, and let her have it when she comes
back ? "

" We'll order her one all to herself,"
Brenda said magnificently ; but the children
were in love with their own plan and wouldn't
hear of anything else.

" It would be your ice, not ours then, you
know, Brenda, and it's got to be ours," they
explained vociferously, and for the sake of
peace Brenda allowed them to ladle rather
sloppy ice on to a cake-plate cleared for the
purpose.   After all, it was probably right
to encourage them to be kind to less lucky
people : Brenda's governesses expected her
to make collections of her more childish toys
and story-books for the Children's Hospitals
at Christmas-time, and always talked about
the beauty of giving.

Florrie was back pretty promptly with the
bill ; evidently Brenda had succeeded in
impressing the need of haste.   Pris and
Penny caught her by the sleeve.   " There's
an ice for you," they cried.   " It's a little

bit of all our ices that Brenda is giving us,
and it's a very extra ice now, because it's
so rotten for you never having any. Sit
down and have it—she can, can't she,
Brenda ? ''

Brenda was rather doubtful. " Perhaps
she would rather have it in her own room,"
she suggested, as poor Florrie took the plate,
half filled with melting strawberry ice, in
which floated currants and crumbs of pastry,
and stared at it quite unbelievingly.

" Much I'd get if I took this here down
to the kitchen ; they'd never believe but
that how I took it," she said hoarsely.

" Oh then, she must have it here, mustn't
she, Brenda ? " Pris, Penny, and Betty all
shrieked at Brenda at the same moment.

" Squeeze your chairs up a bit, and let her
get on to the window-seat," Brenda ordered.
" There you are, Florrie ; give her a cake,
one of you ; make haste and enjoy it before
anybody sends you back to work. I'll take
a long time getting out the money for paying
my bill."

In spite of all these preparations for her
benefit Florrie still seemed unaccountably
tearful ; but Brenda felt sure that she must
be happy really ; and it was a much more
satisfactory way of being kind than that dull

old business of looking up possessions she was supposed to have outgrown, and sending them to hospitals with an appropriate message, because it was the duty of a princess to do that sort of thing.

She was feeling particularly pleased with life, when — something happened ! Three people, a tall man and two rather small boys, came by the shop, and one of the boys pulled up, and raised his cap to Brenda. The other two stopped then, as well ; and the tall man grinned and lifted his hat.

Next moment the grin faded, and just as Brenda had recognised him for Carol's form master, Mr. Reresby, evidently out for a walk with Carol and another boy, he marched explosively into the shop, and addressed himself unceremoniously to the party :

" Go outside at once, please, all you Beech House people, but keep away from my boys ! And you "—he was looking at Florrie— " I don't suppose it's your fault, but you've no right to be out, and with other children. Go home and go to bed ; you've got measles."

CHAPTER XII

THE B. HOUSE CAPTAIN

BRENDA bristled. " Really, Mr. Reresby . . . ! "

" Out ! " Mr. Reresby said, in a tone that really admitted no argument, and Brenda, much to her own surprise, found herself going.

" I haven't paid our bill yet," she objected at the door.

" I'll do that," Mr. Reresby said promptly. " I've had measles."

Brenda gave him her purse. He took it, and spoke from the doorway to the two boys : " Go a bit farther down the street; we don't want Rollincourt in quarantine."

The last words made Brenda distinctly uncomfortable ; she had heard a little from M. M. what was meant by quarantine.

It was a dejected party that waited outside the confectioner's, while Mr. Reresby settled for the feast ; Betty was crying because she hadn't finished her ice, and Pris and Penny were in the depths because poor Florrie hadn't nearly finished hers. Brenda was

annoyed at the dictatorial way in which Mr.
Reresby had removed Carol from her neighbourhood, and anxious too about that un-
pleasant word " quarantine."

And then into the midst of them arrived
Miss Hunt, nearly distracted, and extremely
vexed with Brenda.   It appeared that she
hadn't heard her call, and had been hunting
for the children everywhere, and in any case
it was absolutely against rules to have taken
them into a shop and fed them upon ices or
anything without permission.

" They were *heavenly* ices," Penny said,
at the first pause.   There had not been a
moment in which Brenda could get in her
apology before, and she couldn't help
giggling at Penny's tone of reminiscent
rapture.   That was unfortunate, because
Miss Hunt decided that she was not taking
her offences seriously, and Mr. Reresby took
that opportunity to come out and mention
the measles.   Brenda went back to Beech
House in dire disgrace, and was reported to
Miss Christopherson for breaking rules and
for impertinence.   Brenda's interview with
the Head was not at all agreeable, and she
came away from it in the depths, having
learned that the " Florrie " business meant
that Beech House could meet no other school

at a match till the weeks of quarantine were
ended. Two matches must be scratched
for this week, and two for next, and if any
of the party caught measles the quarantine
might be indefinitely prolonged. Also the
fourteen who had come up against that case
of measles had to live apart from all the
rest till they were safe again. The girls had
been so down upon her for losing five marks
to B. House ; what they would say and do
to a girl who lost Beech House any number
of matches, she really trembled to think.
Miss Christopherson had not left much
stuffing in her ; it would have taken very
little to reduce Brenda to tears.

However, she got to the San. wing, where
the fourteen would have to live just now ; it
was empty, for her fellow-victims were out in
the San. garden. She pulled out her writing-
case, and began a letter to her father :

" BEECH HOUSE,
9th May.

" DEAR FATHER,—I know that you will
think me very foolish, but I should be very
grateful if you would please to reconsider
your decision about school, and have me
home again. I am not getting on at all
well at Beech House, and have just plunged

the school into quarantine, which will make all the girls detest me. . . ."

Somebody spoke outside the open window. " Why aren't you out in the garden instead of sticking in and writing on an evening like this ? " demanded the voice of Margaret Reresby.

Brenda had tears in her eyes ; she was feeling such a hopeless failure, and the letter to her father brought back all the high hopes with which she came to Beech House not a fortnight ago. But she didn't want Margaret to know that fact, and bent down over her desk to look for an unwanted envelope. " I've just finished," she mumbled.

" What are you writing—a letter ? " Margaret asked, with good-natured authority. " It isn't the day for them, you know."

Brenda did not answer : quite suddenly she couldn't. It was too dreadful about the quarantine and its consequences ; of course Margaret didn't know yet, or she wouldn't have spoken so kindly.

" Put your writing away," Margaret said quickly but gently. " I want to talk to you. I was going to ask you to my study this evening, if it hadn't been for this silly business. It's a decent little place ; you'll have one yourself when you get to be a Sixth Former."

" I shan't be staying," Brenda said, rather huskily. She had got hold of herself a little, but it was harder than she expected to speak without breaking down.

" Not staying ? Of course, you will," Margaret said. " No one ever leaves Beech House till they must, I can tell you. I wish I weren't going to be eighteen next term."

" I've put the school into quarantine," Brenda told her tragically, " and it's the match with Saddington next week."

" Yes, I know, and it's a great nuisance," Margaret said candidly. " You were a little silly to do what you did. . . ."

" The girls will never forgive me," Brenda remarked.

" But you're being a worse silly about it all now," Margaret went on, as though she had not spoken. " Nobody supposes that you knew about measles, and the people in the shop were most to blame about that. Why you were so idiotic was in supposing you could cart off crowds of kids and stuff them at your own free will. Why didn't you ask first ? "

" I did call out to Miss Hunt."

" Well, you might have known that wasn't

the way to do it," Margaret remarked
sensibly. " I always thought they taught an
extra lot of manners to you royalties. You
don't call out you're doing something to one
of the Staff ; you go and ask properly if you
may do it. I suppose you just didn't think.
I should let Miss Hunt know that you didn't
understand what you ought to have done, and
are sorry about it : you don't want her to
think you don't learn manners in Nystrea ? "

" No," murmured Brenda, feeling hot.

" As for consequences, of course, they're
unlucky," Margaret went on ; " but you
won't find the girls round on you about
those. You've been rowed for breaking rules,
not for putting the school into quarantine."

" But suppose all those babies get measles
one after another ? " Brenda demanded
desperately.

" Suppose that nothing of the kind happens
—why the dickens should it ? " Margaret
wanted to know. " We've got to be in
quarantine, of course, till the incubation time
is over, and very tiresome it is ; but it's not
nearly so bad as it would have been a little
later in the term, with the big matches coming
on, and the Pageant, and all the rest of it.
And there's no earthly reason to look at the
dark side and settle that we must get measles

because some of us were near it.   Otherwise
we should be always getting chicken-pox and
mumps and things from trains and buses."

" It's very kind of you to talk like this,"
Brenda said, a little comforted.

" I'm only talking sense, and I'll say one
thing more for your benefit, my dear kid ;
and if you remember it, you'll find it much
smoother going at Beech House. Don't be
so keen on going your own way ; if you'll
only believe it, the way that most new girls
go—and that's the way they're advised to go
—is a lot more sensible."

" M. M. did seem to think I oughtn't to
play about with the babies much," Brenda
acknowledged.

" Of course she did, and if you had paid
attention to what she said, you wouldn't
have landed yourself this time," Margaret
reminded her. " But you'll know better
next time ; so just cheer up and get some
tennis practice while you can. There's a
good court in the San. grounds, and I'd like
you to be able to play for the House before
long. Oh, what about your letter ? "

" Oh, I won't send this one, thanks,"
Brenda said, tearing it up. " And I'd simply
love it if I can be good enough to play for
B. House, Margaret."

CHAPTER XIII

THE ENROLMENT

THE day of the Enrolment had come.
Brenda was fairly well broken in to
public ceremonies, though her experience
had been nothing like as large as Carol's.
Also she was quite accustomed to have people
looking at her. She didn't think for one
single instant that she would be nervous,
and had listened with sympathy, but not
much understanding, to the groans of the
other Tenderfoots, who all appeared to be in
what they described as " a blue funk."

" It's all very well for K. to tell us she's
gone through every single thing with us and
we can't go wrong," Sonia said. " It will
all go out of my head when I hear my name
and ' Forward march ! ' I know it will—
and it will be simply ghastly."

" Oh, I don't think it ought to be as bad
as that," Brenda put in. " A District Commissioner isn't such a terrifically alarming
personage, I should imagine."

" Well, anyhow, I shall be thankful when

the Enrolment's over," Nancy said, shivering realistically. (Brenda had an idea that the new girls were piling up the agony a bit.) " P'raps *you* don't know what it feels like to go down in a lift too fast, when you haven't had anything to eat for ages, and—are going to the dentist's."

" Do you ? " asked Brenda.

" Well, not p'raps all of it at once," Nancy acknowledged, " but I know that is about what the Enrolment will be like—I mean the beginning before one's enrolled."

Brenda had laughed then ; now, as she stood in her place in the Horseshoe among the " Swallows," in uniform, but with tie hanging loose and no shoulder-knot as yet, and heard the little stir in the hall announcing the arrival of the District Commissioner, she suddenly felt her mouth go dry. She was just a Tenderfoot ; she felt scared stiff, and in the mere fact of being a princess there was no help at all !

Steps outside, and breath held in the Horseshoe ; Miss Kean had her eyes fixed rigidly on the door, ready to give the order, " Company, salute ! " the very instant that Miss Ferrars ushered in the District Commissioner. Every one seemed to be suffering a little from a sense of being screwed up tight.

The door opening : Patrol Leaders, all inside the Horseshoe and each standing in front and at the exact centre of her Patrol, cast one anxious glance behind to make sure that the Patrol was in perfect alignment— smartness of kit had all been looked to earlier, and there wasn't a stocking-seam so much as a hairbreadth askew—before freezing to rigid attention at the " Company, *alert* ! " from the Lieutenant.

The District Commissioner walked in. The Captain's order came clear and ringing, " Company, salute ! " and the hand of every enrolled Guide flew up in the Guide salute.

The Commissioner returned the salute, and took her place at the opening of the Horseshoe, the Captain on her left, and Miss Kean on her right. Miss Kean had the shoulder-knots marking the differing Patrols on a little table beside her ; the Captain, the little gleaming metal Guide brooches, of no intrinsic value, and yet, for what they represent, the most valuable of her possessions to each Guide.

The new Guides for the Swallows were to be the last enrolled : in that dreadful minute of panic when Guides and Tenderfoots waited for the Commissioner, Brenda had felt quite relieved to know that she herself would not have to do anything for quite a long time; now she felt that she wanted the moment to come when that little trefoil brooch would be hers and she would receive from the Commissioner the handshake of a comrade, and be able to return the salute of the Company—one of them, not one alone, as she was at home in Nystrea.

But the Enrolment was beginning; Brenda remembered that she must stand to attention, though not yet a Guide. Three to be enrolled before her from the Robins, one from the Wrens, one from the Canaries, two from the Thrushes, all before Sonia, Nancy, and herself became Guides and members of the Swallow Patrol. The first of the Tenderfoots was marching up now, looking red and shy, but keeping step manfully with her Patrol Leader, Glenna Graham, C. House Captain.

" Do you promise on your honour . . ."

.   .   .   .   .   .

It was Brenda's turn. " Brenda of Nystrea, forward march ! "

Brenda fell into line with Katharine-Ursula, and marched up to the Commissioner. She did not feel so scared now, for the Commissioner's eyes were very kind.

" Do you promise on your honour . . ."
" I promise on my honour . . ."

" I trust you on your honour to keep this promise."

The left handclasp of the Guide, a firm, steady handclasp that had meaning in it ; the Swallow shoulder-knot adjusted by Katharine, the Guide brooch pinned into the centre of her tie.

" Salute the Colours ! "

That had always thrilled Brenda ; your first salute as a Guide given to the King's Colours. She stood sideways to salute those Colours, as they were carried immovably by Margaret, with Judy Kerne and Betty Savage forming the guard of honour. Then the Commissioner turned her to face the Company.

" Brenda of Nystrea is now a full member of the Sisterhood of the Guides."

" Company, salute ! " That was Miss Ferrars, and Brenda gave and received the full salute of the Guides.

Nancy and Sonia followed her ; and then the National Anthem was sung, the full Company at the salute, and the Colours were marched off, with the salute, held till they had been lowered in the adjoining room.

The Commissioner gave the order " Sit," in the most genial of tones, and everybody thankfully relaxed. The Commissioner made a step forward, and looked round at the huge blue Horseshoe with a smile. She spoke for two minutes, at the end of which she stopped, rather abruptly. Brenda thought enviously how much easier it would be to be good, if they occasionally talked to her at home about the things she might do, instead of the many things she mightn't. Then she pulled herself up. After all, her father had allowed her to come to school, and the girls had been very decent to her about that quarantine business, which might have been so serious if any of the party had developed measles. Luckily nobody had, but Brenda had been really grateful for the girls' forbearance.

She joined with a will in the cheers for which the Captain called, and afterwards in the Inter-Patrol Competition Game, when each Patrol had to prepare a " camp " in ten minutes, labelling everything to show what it was intended to represent, and putting it in the right position. The Commissioner, the Captain, and Lieutenant walked round the camps at the end of the ten minutes, marking for correctness of detail, completeness, position, and ingenuity of arrangement. Katharine and M. M. made for a corner of the garden, and while M. M. wrote out with lightning speed the names of various camp

possessions on pages torn from the little note-
book she carried in a pocket of her tunic,
K. worked out the points of the compass,
decided which way the wind blew—there
wasn't much—and sent her Patrol flying for
chairs to represent the tents.

Ten minutes isn't long in which to prepare
even a camp where there are no real tents to
pitch, and no real stores to arrange, or grease-
pits to dig; and only two of the Swallows
had really camped. But everybody worked,
and when the Captain's whistle sounded the
order to " Cease work," chairs, flower-pots,
stones, and leaves were all representing
something wanted in a camp and placed carefully in the right positions. Sonia had forgotten that the grease-pit should be handy to
the washing-up place, and had labelled the
wrong flower-pot " grease-pit," and Brenda
had arranged a tent opening on the wrong
side; but otherwise the camp was a very
creditable ten minutes' work, considering that
almost everything used in it had to be
fetched from the house or tool-shed.

And the Swallows topped the competition
by one mark. Brenda enjoyed that Enrolment Day, and had a comfortable feeling
that school life would turn out all that she
had dreamed it, now she was a Guide.

CHAPTER XIV

THE STOP-GAP

"HEARD the news, Brenda ? "
    " No. What ? "
    " Miss Kean's gone away—her mother's frightfully ill, and she was phoned for last night ever so late. Miss Christopherson sent her in a taxi to the junction, and she got the express."

    " Poor thing. Do you think her mother's going to die, M. M. ? " asked Brenda. " What is it ? "

    " K. thought pneumonia, but Miss Christopherson didn't tell her much about Mrs. Kean, only about who'll take our form and all that."

    " Who is going to ? "

    " Oh, it's pretty rotten—we've got to have that feeble little thing, Miss Peterkin, who took IIA for a week last term."

    " Don't know the lady," observed Brenda.

    " No, of course you weren't here ; but you must have seen her the other day. She was in to tea, sitting with the IIA's—rather a lost sort of expression, and walks like a moorhen, with her head poked forward."

"They're not going to put us off with *that*!" Brenda cried.

"They are—at least Miss Christopherson is. She told K. so."

"But why on earth——? "

"Well, I suppose Peterkin is on the spot; she lives with an aunt who is the widow of a defunct vicar of this place—she *would* be!— and Miss Christopherson doesn't want to get any one down here from Truman's without knowing how long Keany is likely to be away. . . . There's the prayer bell!"

Brenda and M. M. hurried to their places in School Hall, thoroughly annoyed with Fate, and inclined to vent at least some of their annoyance on the Stop-Gap. M. M., though not infrequently snubbed by Miss Kean, was much more of an adorer than she cared to acknowledge; and Brenda thoroughly enjoyed the vigorous teaching, so different from the rather dull way in which learning was pumped into her at the Palace (where every governess had been trained to observe the strict traditions hedging round the education of the daughters of the Royal House), and liked getting that occasional word of praise that was so hard to win. It was

horrid to think of anybody in Miss Kean's
place. But there Miss Peterkin was, sure
enough, scuttling ungracefully towards the
form mistress' desk, with her head—a head
that looked queer and old-fashioned, with
dulled fair hair, done in a sort of bun behind
and " endy " about the ears—pushed a little
forward, in the way that M. M. had compared
to a moorhen.

M. M. wrote " Isn't she ? " on her exercise-
book, and passed it to Brenda, who giggled.

" Now, girls, please behave," Miss Peterkin
said, and every girl in IVʙ knew that it was
the wrong sort of beginning.

Botany was the first lesson this morning,
and Miss Kean was particularly good at
botany. The Stop-Gap would have chal-
lenged comparison in any case, and she had
never taken any form as senior as IVʙ.
She meant to interest her form from the
beginning by talking brightly ; unluckily the
brightness was felt to be insulting by a form
which was not disposed to be merciful in its
judgments.

" Seed fruits," she said. " Will one of
you girls in the front row put out the specimens in a row on my desk, and don't eat
any of them, will you ? "

She laughed a little herself in a nervous,

deprecating sort of way, but there was a stony silence from IVB. Only M. M. got up, looking bored, and, taking the specimens of seed fruits, ready quartered from their box, set them out on the desk as desired.

" Now what shall we take first ? " Miss Peterkin was perseveringly bright. " I suppose somebody can tell me what seed fruits are, by the way ? "

She looked round invitingly. Nobody answered.

" Come, IVB girls, surely somebody knows that ? " she said.

M. M. spoke wearily: " Oh, sorry, Miss Peterkin; I thought you were just stating a fact when you made that remark about seed fruit."

" That will do. Don't be impertinent," Miss Peterkin said, growing pink.

" Next girl, please ? "

Judy Kerne gave the desired information, in a voice of which the boredom was modelled on Mariota's. Call this a botany lesson— and M. M. had been set down as though she were a kindergarten kid ! The form resented that, and made no attempt to conceal their resentment. Such replies as Miss Peterkin did get were supremely uninterested.

Brenda herself did not attempt to answer

anything. Having decided within the first
two or three minutes that there was nothing
she could learn from Miss Peterkin, she had
taken her poetry book out of her desk, and
was refreshing her memory before Elocution
Class, which came just after break. A
visiting mistress taught Elocution at Beech
House, and taught it very well ; Brenda
enjoyed that lesson, and thought she could
get on well ahead with her preparation of it,
if she kept the book out of sight on her
knee.

But unluckily she was too much interested
in a dramatic bit to hear, when Miss Peterkin,
observing her bent head, suddenly fired a
direct question at her :

" You, please—the girl at the end—front
row."

M. M. nudged Brenda, and nudged her
hard, and the poetry book fell on the floor.
It made a considerable clatter.

" What are you doing with a book ? "
Miss Peterkin demanded. " Hand it up to
me, please."

Brenda got up and handed it in silence.

." Poetry ? " said Miss Peterkin, looking
at the back. " What were you doing with
a poetry book in a Botany Class ? "

" Reading it, Miss Peterkin," Brenda ex-

plained. " For something to do," she added
in justification.

M. M. exploded absolutely, and without
possibility of concealment, though she did
try to bury her face in her sleeve. Stifled
giggles came from other desks; the form
was thoroughly out of hand.

Miss Peterkin, very pink indeed, asserted
herself. " Silence, please. If I have to
speak again, there will be a conduct mark
for everybody. You, please, what is your
name ? "

" Brenda, Miss Peterkin."

" Well, Brenda, you want something to do,
apparently. You may stand here at my
desk, and take the botany lesson, till I tell
you to leave off. I am surprised that a
Girl Guide, as I see you are by your badge,
should not wish to behave better."

Brenda saw M. M. stiffen at this last
speech ; then she looked very straight at
Brenda, standing beside the Stop-Gap's desk.
Brenda, who had been upon the point of
apologising, read that look aright. M. M.
meant, " Stick it out." Brenda felt distinctly nervous, and as if the little botany
she knew had all deserted her; but the
remark about the Guides had rasped her too,
and she sensed that the form was with her.

" Certainly," she said, speaking as coolly as possible, though her mouth was dry. " I shall be delighted."

She stepped up on the little dais, and took up one of the specimens—a pomegranate.

" We will pass the specimens round next," she said blandly, " and I should like to hear what every one notices for herself."

Miss Peterkin stood silent and rather helpless. She had probably expected, Brenda guessed, that the rebel would apologise humbly for her impertinence, rather than face the taking of the class before a mistress ; the last thing that she dreamed of was that Brenda would accept the suggestion calmly, and think of something that meant no effort on her part. Brenda chuckled inwardly as she saw the expression on the Stop-Gap's face.

The form wouldn't let her down, she knew that. She leaned her elbow on the desk, and waited placidly, while M. M. and Judy took round the specimens, and M. M. led off with a well-observed and clear description of the peculiarities of the pomegranate. She took her time over it too, and evidently was out to give the tip to the rest. There were twelve specimens ; it seemed that, with judicious management, their de-

scription would take up the remainder of
the lesson quite easily.

Miss Peterkin's intended punishment had
fallen very flat, and Brenda had come out
the victor, but she didn't feel quite as
triumphant as she had expected. Perhaps
it was the tired, hopeless look upon the Stop-
Gap's face that made her feel as though it
had been rather a poor thing to score as she
had done.

It was a relief when Miss Peterkin said,
"That will do; sit down, please," and
resumed the lesson. Brenda paid attention
for the remainder of the hour, though it
wasn't particularly easy, because her defeat
seemed to have taken from poor Miss
Peterkin what little power of being interesting she possessed.

IVb were to join IVa for maths, the next
class; Brenda went out with the others,
but at the door turned back.

"Miss Peterkin, I'm very sorry I was
rude," she said, in a low voice, hoping that
the rest of the form wouldn't think her going
back on them.

Miss Peterkin quite jumped, and looked
as though it wouldn't take a great deal to
make her cry.

"Thank you; that is nice of you." Then

in a burst of confidence, " I dare say my
teaching does seem poor and stupid after
Miss Kean's — but I did want to manage
this week that Miss Christopherson asked me
to take, if I could. . . . But I shall have to
tell her . . . I have been used to younger
girls, you see ; and now I hear that one of
the girls is a princess, and that will make it
all more difficult . ."

Brenda interrupted at this point ; she was
feeling smaller and more ashamed of herself
than she had ever done in all her life before.
The fact that she had scored so beautifully
off Miss Peterkin did not seem a subject of
congratulation any longer, nor did it matter
so frightfully that she had been irritating
about Guides.

" I am really very sorry indeed," she
repeated; " but please don't worry or think
we are going to be difficult. I was much the
worst, you know—and I shan't be again.
And I wouldn't bother the least bit about
the princess—she's just an ordinary Beech
House girl."

Brenda flew, and was rebuked for coming
in late to the maths class. But she felt a
comfortable conviction that she had been
late in a good cause, and did not worry. In
break, she got M. M., Judy, and Peggy

Wantage together, and told them as much as seemed fair to repeat of Miss Peterkin's confession.

" So we can't go on being horrid to her," she said firmly.

" I suppose we can't," sighed M. M.

" It seems a pity we know, doesn't it ? Why did you linger so officiously behind ? And why, if it comes to that, did she shove girl-guiding down our throats, and so make the devil enter into me ? I shouldn't have urged you to that last stunt, if it hadn't been for that."

" It was a brainy stunt," chuckled Judy. " I've no objection to pax now, as we scored, thanks to Brenda. What shall we do— general subscrip. and a bunch of roses got in the school walk, I think, and M. M. to give them."

" No—Brenda," said M. M.

" Yes," agreed practically all the form, and Brenda found, to her immense surprise, that the proceeding which she had thought would probably annoy the form, seemed in some mysterious way to have sent up her prestige, in a way that all her best efforts had failed to do.

She presented the big bunch of crimson roses to Miss Peterkin in the name of the form, when they came back from the school walk, and heard that they would be so lovely for " Aunt Emilia," who had been crippled with rheumatism for weeks, and couldn't get out. Brenda wondered if Aunt Emilia's rheumatism might have been part of the reason that her niece was so anxious to be able to manage the teaching of IVB for the week of Miss Kean's absence, and determined that, at least as far as she was concerned, Miss Peterkin should find that she could manage.

And as M. M. felt the same, IVB came into line, and Miss Peterkin made a most successful stop-gap.

CHAPTER XV

AN·URGENT PROBLEM

IT was the Sunday that came in the middle
of Miss Peterkin's week, a hot, airless
Sunday. There had been a special preacher
in the morning, and he had preached for
forty-three minutes, carefully timed by quite
half a hot and indignant school, which
thought ten minutes ample for a sermon.
Every one was feeling rather tired and
cross, for there had been a hustle to get
ready for dinner, instead of the usual
pleasant laze in the garden, and when the
after-dinner hour of letter-writing came, the
girls were more inclined to grumble than to
write.

Katharine-Ursula, M. M., Peggy Wantage,
and Brenda had made a little screened-off
place of their own, with rugs hung over the
branches of two trees and safety-pinned
together, leaving one side open. Miss Hunt,
who passed that way, laughed a little, and
wanted to know why they chose such an
airless afternoonfor shutting themselves in ;

but then grown-up people never did see the advantage of a private place.

They were very cosy there—just the four of them, with their writing-cases—and delightfully private; and if they were a little hotter than they need have been, that was certainly their own affair and nobody else's.

Brenda at least put down the heat to quite another cause.

" Oh, this *horrible* hair ! " she groaned, as her thick curls flopped over her hot face when she turned over on her front to begin her letter.   " It gets a worse nuisance every day."

" Tell your father so in your letter," suggested M. M.   " It will be something to say."

" Won't he let you be shingled ? " suggested Peggy.   " You'd look awfully nice shingled, really, wouldn't she, K. ?   Curly hair and the right-shaped head."

" Your father objects, doesn't he ? " asked Katharine, looking up from the letter she had begun, and discreetly waiving the question as to whether shingling would suit Brenda.

Brenda pushed her hair back viciously. " Object ?   I should think he does !   Hates shingling like poison—at least that's what

he gives me to understand. I don't believe
he has any idea what it looks like really ! "

"Send him a snap of *Me* ! " suggested
M. M., striking an attitude.

" It's all that bothering tradition,"
grumbled Brenda. " His bothering aunts
and everybody had long hair when they were
my age. I shouldn't mind so much if it
were straight and could be plaited ; but he
won't have that because of the curliness."

" It is hard lines on you," Katharine said.
She might have added that it was hard lines
on her ; she brushed Brenda's hair and tied
it back for her nine mornings out of ten, or
Brenda would have been sent up to Matron,
disgraced. It meant getting up at least ten
minutes earlier for Katharine, and what was
worse, getting Brenda up ; but Princess
Brenda had never done her own hair in her
life before she came to school, and had taken
a neatness mark twice a day regularly while
K. was sleeping in the sick-room.

" Oh, well, if your pater is like that about
hair, I shouldn't ask him ; I should just get
it shingled, and tell him the deed was done,"
M. M. said calmly. " That's what I did ;
my father used to pull my hair, and had a
sentimental fancy he liked it long. I told
him I wanted it shingled, and he said,

' Rubbish! You only think you do.' So I just showed him it was more than thinking."

" What happened ? " Brenda asked.

" Nothing much. Nothing can, when the thing's done. There was a little bit of a storm, but I kept calm, and it blew over. That's the way to manage—to keep calm about these episodes ; they don't go on rowing you, if you don't answer back, and they get used to the shingle in two-two's and only pretend they mind it."

" Don't go putting Brenda up to doing anything of the kind," Katharine said decidedly. " It's different for her."

" Would it be a sort of high treason if you went against your father, Brenda ? " asked Peggy.

" I don't know—no, of course it couldn't be. I don't think for a moment that he would notice—he doesn't see me much, and I don't suppose he cares how I look really. Only he has got that idea that shingled hair is too modern or something silly. I'd like to make him wear my hair for a week or two, and see how he liked it."

" I don't suppose he knows what a bother it is at school," Katharine said. " Why don't you just ask him whether, now you are a Beech House girl, he would mind ? "

" ' Dear Father, may I ask if you will be
so very kind as to graciously reconsider
your views about my hair ? ' " Brenda said,
with exaggerated deference. " And in three
or four days I should get a dictated letter
back :

" ' You should be old enough to know that
my decisions are once and for all. Do not
refer again to the subject of your hair,
please,' and that would be that."

" Would it be that, if you really explained
to him about school, and what a trial your
kind of hair is ? " Katharine wanted to
know.

" Oh, Father wouldn't bother to understand anything about me," Brenda said
impatiently. " If I'm ever to get shingled
hair, it will have to be M. M.'s way "

" We've only got a little over half an hour
for our letters," warned Peggy, who had not
the pen of a ready writer, and knew that
her mother liked four sides.

" Good-night ! " exclaimed M. M., and
began to scribble at her fastest and blottiest
rate.

Brenda sat up, cross-legged : it was no
good trying to write comfortably lying down,
as the others were doing. Her hair would
do nothing but get in the way, and her

father was extremely critical of her handwriting.

What in the world was she to say to him ?
The others were all writing away vigorously,
but then they were writing to their mothers,
and didn't have to discard half the everyday happenings of life, as not suitable or not
likely to be approved.

" DEAR FATHER,—The weather has been
quite hot again for the last week, and my
form has been allowed to bathe three times."

Brenda considered this first sentence carefully, then scratched out the " for," and
wrote " during " over it ; then decided that
it wouldn't do to send a letter with any
erasure in it, and took another sheet.

" DEAR FATHER,—The weather has been
quite hot again during the last week, and my
form has been allowed to bathe three times,
which was very agreeable.

" The Guide Company, in which I am now
enrolled, competes with the Guide Companies in the district for a swimming cup,
on a date fixed towards the end of July. It
will be very nice if our Company should be
fortunate enough to win it.

" In lessons, my form is taking the reign

of Queen Anne, both in its historical and literary aspect, which is very interesting ; the geography of Scotland and its influence upon the national character, and . . ."

" Bit of a slowcoach, aren't you, Brenda ? " remarked M. M., who had finished, and wanted to talk.   " I've written two sheets of a big block, and told Mummy all the news, while you've been pumping out that little bit."

" P'raps you'd like to see the kind of letters I have to write, and then you'll see why I'm not quick at them," Brenda said, rather bitterly.   " I could write fast enough if I was writing to some one who wanted to hear all the little things."

M. M. read the letter soberly, and whistled. " A bit stodgy, isn't it ? " she commented candidly.   " No wonder you're a bit slow over an effusion of that sort.   Poor old thing !   How were you going to finish ? "

" There is no more news, so I will conclude. —Your affectionate and dutiful daughter,
                    " BRENDA."
Brenda said grimly.

" Good-night ! " ejaculated M. M.   " It doesn't seem worth while to have wasted nearly half an hour on a letter like that."

" I could do as good a one as yours in ten minutes if——" fired Brenda.

She snatched her pad, tore off the unfinished letter, and scribbled furiously :

" DEAREST FATHER,—I've only got ten minutes, because we've been jawing and ragging in our letter-hour, so please forgive a frightful scribble. I've so much to say, that unless I write like mad I shan't be able to tell you half.

" What *do* you think ? I'm in the trial four who will probably swim for the Cup Isn't that topping ? And I've only just been enrolled as a Guide, too. I *do* hope I shan't get thrown out, but anyhow I shall have been in the running.

" The Cup happens at the end of term, when there is a big Rally, and one Company wins the Shield—don't you hope it's us, and *couldn't* you come over for it ? It would be topping to have you and show you everybody, specially M. M. and Katharine-Ursula.

" I can't stop to tell you about lessons ; but, oh, Father, couldn't you stop being old-fashioned about my hair, for I'm sure you don't like me to get as many neatness marks as I do for not being properly brushed. If you'll let me have it off, I'll let it grow when I leave school, and life isn't so rushed.

" Carol seems to be getting on awfully well, and looks much fitter and ever so brown. . . ."

A bell rang violently. " Come on," said Katharine, scrambling to her feet. " That means letters handed in, you know, and Miss Christopherson wants us at three to-day instead of five past, so that she can finish the book."

There was a wild confusion; everybody except K. had forgotten the fact that there wouldn't to-day be the usual five minutes' grace. Peggy was blotting her letter, and imploring the loan of an envelope from some one; Katharine and M. M. were unpinning and folding rugs. Brenda addressed an envelope to her father, and then found she had mislaid her letter; rummaged desperately, was told by Katharine, " You *must* come," caught a glimpse of her handwriting on a crumpled sheet of paper, which Peggy had knelt upon, and thrust it into the envelope; then gathered up her writing-case and papers, without waiting to straighten these out. As it was, there was only just time to hand in her letter to Miss Hunt and get to Miss Christopherson, in her private part of the garden, where the Upper School always went to listen to her reading on summer Sunday afternoons when the weather allowed.

. . . .

On Monday afternoon, it so happened it was " Hair," for IVB. Shampooing for all, cutting and singeing for those who required it. The necessary number of rooms and attendants had been bespoken for the hour of 3.30, and IVB marched down in good spirits, pleased to feel that they were missing almost an hour of prep and had nothing before them but " Hair," tea, and an evening of games.

Miss Peterkin was in charge, and was obviously nervous, it being the first time of taking what the girls called " Hair-Parade." It hadn't been the " Hair " week for IIA when she had them last term.

" Do you all know what you are to have done ? " she fussed, as the croc came in sight of the hairdressing establishment.

" Rather, Miss Peterkin ; don't you worry any," M. M. said kindly, and her form left her planted upon a plush-covered sofa in the passage of the upstairs hairdressing saloon, with moderately recent copies of *The Queen* and *Punch* to keep her entertained while waiting for the girls.

It was the first time that Brenda had ever gone to an ordinary hairdressing establishment, and she enjoyed the experience : at the Palace a highly certificated personage came up once in six weeks and did all that was needed for her hair, and her maid and one of her governesses were always present, and she had about as much say in the proceedings as a wax doll.

Here everything was new and interesting : the funny little compartments, the advertisements, the description of various dyes, the disclaimers of responsibility for the same ; the scale of prices ; the neat, bright girl, with beautifully dressed hair and a spotless white overall, who called her " Miss."

" Shampoo, Miss ? Yes ; and cut and singed as well ? "

She took off Brenda's hair ribbon, and arrayed a sort of white cloak round her shoulder under her mane of hair.

" How much will you have off, Miss ? "

" I'd like it all off ! " Brenda said.

" Not a shingle, Madam, surely, with all that lovely hair," remonstrated the attendant. " Though, of course, it is difficult to look smart with it long in these days—it being all the fashion to show the shape of the head."

M. M.'s words of yesterday shot through Brenda's head as the attendant stood, scissors in hand, waiting to hear what she wanted.

Why not ? There was nobody to interfere, and when the hair was off, it was off. It would be too gorgeous to be free of that constant worry ; of " neatness marks " that scored against her House ; of all that hustle in the morning when she might stay in bed till the last five minutes, as M. M. did. Miss Peterkin would not say anything ; she did not know what the girls were supposed to have done this afternoon, and for once in her life she was free of supervision and able to give her own orders. The girls evidently thought it the sensible sort of thing—to get it done, and stand the racket. M. M.'s father hadn't minded long, and he really liked M. M.'s long hair if he was accustomed to pull it. *Her* father had never shown that he liked anything of hers, or seemed to want to give her pleasure.

" I'll have it——" Brenda began, and then gave pause.

Father had let her come to school, though it wasn't the education he approved ; he had given her her own way then, and that at least showed some kindness and some trust. Perhaps it was letting down that kindness and that trust if she took advantage of her freedom to have her hateful hair off without his permission. Like M. M., Brenda had intensely resented Miss Peterkin's unfortunate remark about Guides on her first class with IVв, but that didn't prevent her from having her own idea of a Guide's honour, which was to be trusted, though it was a thing one wouldn't talk about.

" I'll have it—just tipped and singed and shampooed," she said.

CHAPTER XVI

PREPARING THE PAGEANT

MISS CHRISTOPHERSON had visitors to tea, IVʙ observed, as they "crocked" past the drawing-room windows; but they had no idea that the visitors were anything to concern them, until they came out into the garden with Miss Christopherson and Miss Ferrars.

The girls had had tea by that time, and were settling to tennis, or to looking on and waiting their turn for the courts.

Brenda and M. M. were on the bank above one of the courts, watching Margaret, who was to represent Beech House at the Inter-School Tournament, when they heard their names called by Miss Ferrars, "Brenda! Mariota!" and, scrambling up the bank in a hurry, found themselves facing the Divisional and the District Commissioners, out of uniform but rather awe-inspiring all the same.

"This is Brenda of Nystrea, Lady Stanhope—a new Guide," Miss Christopherson said; " and this is Mariota Mountnessing, quite an old one."

Both Commissioners shook hands with the girls, and then sat down on the bank, and proceeded to explain why they were wanted.

The second half of the great Guide Rally, which took place towards the end of July, was to consist in an historical pageant, representing heroic girlhood through the ages. Each episode was to be given into the hands of one Guide Company; and Miss Christopherson was willing to let the Beech House Guides undertake the charming cavalier scene in which Mistress Diana Chetwynd, aged fourteen, played the King's Protector, for all the objections of her pusillanimous father and a troop of Roundheads searching everywhere for the young King.

" He was hiding in a hay-loft," Lady Stanhope said, " and his description and that of the clothes he wore, together with the penalty imposed on any who sheltered or helped him to escape, was posted at the blacksmith's forge. Diana found him when looking for a strayed kitten, and saw that he must be captured if she could not get him out of the suspected neighbourhood, and along to her great-uncle's old Manor at Ferrybridge, ten miles away, which abounded in hiding-places. Old Sir Nicholas Chetwynd, though too old and infirm to have fought at Worcester, was the staunchest of Royalists, and there was no doubt that the King would be safe in his keeping, could she get him there. Her father locked her into her room for fear she should do anything that might give offence to the Roundheads, but the plucky child climbed out of the window, stole the livery of the man who usually attended her upon her rides, and a huge cranberry pie that she had herself made that morning, and crept to the stable-loft.

" King Charles ii. disguised himself as best he could, while Mistress Diana saddled two horses below (she seems to have been a very all-round competent young person), and then she and her groom set out boldly, with no attempt at concealment, to ride through the village, and across the bridge guarded by Roundhead troopers; the child in front and the King behind, in the Chetwynd livery, and with a great basket on his arm, containing the cranberry pie." The Commissioner paused.

"I say, wasn't she a sport ? " M. M. cried enthusiastically, and Brenda was no less interested. She had always liked the Civil

War period in English history. "Do please go on; did they get through?"

"They got through the village without Diana's absence being discovered by her father, but were held up at the bridge by a certain Corporal Hate-Sin Hazelton—I like their names, don't you? He apparently had his suspicions, and refused to let the groom pass without reference to his superior officer. That would probably have been the end of it as far as the King was concerned; but he and Diana between them were equal to the emergency.

"'If oi stays, t'poi stays,' said the King, who had been breaking off corners of it and putting them into his mouth all the time the Corporal was refusing to let him past the bridge; and he plunged off his horse and propped himself against the bridge rail, and took out a clasp-knife, as though all he cared about were to eat.

"Diana acted, too, as though the pie were all that mattered. She flew at her pretended groom, and boxed his ears with all her strength for spoiling her beautiful handiwork—such big, ripe cranberries, and such short, rich crust—there would never be such another cranberry pie! Of course she made the soldiers want to taste it, as she intended, and the long and short of it was that the horses were tethered to the bridge rail, and the Roundhead soldiers sat down to sample the pie before sending to their superior officer to know his pleasure about the passing of the young lady and her groom. The pie was so good that they simply could not tear themselves away from it, and a village lad, a faithful friend of Diana's, recognising her sign, crept near and loosed the horses. Both were on their backs, lying low in the saddle, and across the bridge, before the soldiers had realised that the horses could be loose, and were out of shot range before they had recovered their scattered wits, or Corporal Hazelton's mouth was empty enough to shout an order to fire. Diana brought the King safely to Ferrybridge, and to this very day a cranberry pie forms the staple dish at table on the anniversary of the King's escape."

"What a lovely story! Thank you ever so much for telling us," Brenda said politely; and M. M. added, "I *am* glad that's our Company scene; but, please, who does what?"

"We have all been talking it over—Lady Stanhope, and Miss Lester, and your Captain, and Margaret Reresby, and myself—over tea,"

Miss Christopherson said, " and the principal
parts are arranged. We think, Brenda, my
dear, that if your father has no objection,
you would make a capital Diana Chetwynd.
I know that you have always ridden, and
your hair is just right for a cavalier girl. . . ."

" Oh, Miss Christopherson, I'm *sure* Father
wouldn't mind my doing anything the others
do," Brenda cried, thrilled.

" We will ask ; but I do not think he would
object," Miss Christopherson said. " Margaret Reresby will be the King—she is dark,
and always the strength of our school
theatricals ; Mariota we thought would be
an excellent boy—Peter is his name ; and
Katharine might be your maid Charity,
Brenda. The parts of Roundhead soldiers
will naturally be taken by the Seniors. . . . I
need not keep you any longer, girls, but I
am sure I can rely upon you to do your very
best to make a great success of our scene in
the Pageant."

" Rather, Miss Christopherson," that was
M. M.

" Thank you ever so much for letting me
be in it," Brenda added ; and the two withdrew, feeling almost indifferent to the chances
of a tennis court.

" Topping both being in it ! " M. M. said ;

" and won't it be *it* playing with Margaret ?
It's the chance of our lives ! "

.   .   .   .

Miss Christopherson, as requested, should
any doubtful point arise with regard to
Princess Brenda's doings, applied to Count
Wrynder on the question of her acting; and
was told that King Conrad was satisfied
that she should do anything that Miss
Christopherson approved. And so, about a
week after the visit of the Commissioners,
she had the thrill of receiving a typewritten
part, a thing which had never happened to
her in her life before. There had been no
acting of any kind for her in Nystrea.

She also received at the same time a letter
from her father, which she read with great
and growing surprise. For King Conrad
said :

" Your bright and spontaneous letter gave
me a great deal of pleasure, my dear Brenda,
and I suppose it is hardly fair to mention
that the writing left something to be desired.
This last letter gave me a far better idea
of your life and surroundings than all which
have gone before, and I am delighted to
know that you are happy at school and
making friends.

" Don't add more slang than you can help
to your vocabulary, though I know that it
is difficult to avoid these short-cuts to one's
meaning, when young. I can make no
promises at this stage, but it would give
me much pleasure to come to your Guide
Rally and see your school.—Your affectionate

" FATHER."

The letter that Brenda had shown to M. M.
could hardly be accused of spontaneity ;
Brenda flew for her writing-case. And there,
crumpled into a corner of it, was the little
letter that she had meant to send. Clearly
she had sent the wrong one : the letter she
had scribbled in ten minutes to show that
she could equal M. M.'s letter-writing pace,
if she could write as other girls did to their
homes.

But it seemed—surprisingly—that her
father really preferred that kind of letter,
in spite of the scribbling and the slang. It
would certainly be a good deal easier to
write to him in future ; Brenda felt suddenly
glad that she had not shingled her hair.

.   .   .   .   .   .

The first rehearsal on the Pageant-ground
took place about a fortnight after the visit

of the Commissioners, and Margaret and
Brenda had orders to attend it in riding kit.
The riding-master who supplied mounts to
Beech House was to bring a couple of
reliable horses which wouldn't be upset by
a little noise, and the rehearsal at the
old stone bridge, which still crossed the
river, was evidently to be done with
" props " complete.

The Beech House performers " crocked "
up to the Pageant-ground in charge of Miss
Ferrars—Brenda and presumably Margaret,
too, feeling a shade self-conscious at walking
with the rest in riding clothes, even though
they were one upon each side of Miss
Ferrars.

Thirty-two Beech House girls were taking
part in the Pageant—twenty-two Guides and
ten Brownies ; the latter were to open proceedings with a country dance on the village
green, which was interrupted by the Roundhead soldiers come to search the neighbourhood for the King.   Pris and Penny were
among the number, and their intense importance was a sight to behold. They
seemed to have an idea that the whole
Pageant rested on their small shoulders. The
pair of them were walking together at the
end of the croc just in front of Miss Ferrars

and her companions, and their conversation
was quite audible. Margaret grinned across
at Brenda. " We'd better take example,
young Diana," she said, and Brenda felt a
thrill of pleasure. Margaret had spoken in
such a nice " equal " tone, for all she was
B. House Captain and a very great personage, and Brenda, a new girl, only IVв,
and a girl who had lost marks to her house,
and plunged the whole school into quarantine
for a fortnight of the most important term.
It *was* nice of Margaret ; the prospect of
acting with her, which had been a shade
alarming, became altogether delightful all
at once.

" I hope I shall be all right," she said.
" I've never acted."

" Realisation of your part is what matters
most in a Pageant," Miss Ferrars said. " It
is frightfully hard for the strongest voice to
carry to a big crowd over big spaces in the
open air ; but you have all your movements
to convey your meaning, and you and
Margaret will have to remember that, all
the time. It shouldn't be too difficult ;
after all, episodes like the capture and escape
at the bridge don't need much talking to
explain them, and should be tremendously
effective."

" Always supposing that the King doesn't pitch off at the critical moment," Margaret said, grinning. " You're all right that way, Brenda, I suppose ; *I* must have some more riding lessons before the great day ! "

CHAPTER XVII

OFF TO CAMP

THE number of Guides for the camp which Miss Ferrars was running for the first week-end in July was strictly limited to forty. Patrol Leaders went, of course, and seconds, and that only left space for two other Guides from each Patrol.

Brenda had very little hope of being among the chosen, though she had been working so hard at guiding that she had already passed her second class, and proudly sewn the little green badge on her right sleeve. But so new a Guide would never be given the chance over the heads of girls who had been in the Patrol for ages; she realised that, and tried to be philosophic when Katharine and M. M., as, of course, they had to do, discussed camping plans at going-to-bed and getting-up times. It all sounded so jolly and unusual and free; and she would be horribly dull at school for that long week-end, with her special friends gone, and a solitary bed-room again, as in Nystrea.

Brenda did try to be bright and interested about the camping plans, and not show she minded; she owed that much to K. and M. M., who had been so decent to her, she considered; but it wasn't too easy a business.

The camp site was about twelve miles away; the Guides got there in two open lorries, which carried themselves and their kit quite easily. Brenda had never been in a lorry in her life, and thought it sounded glorious.

The camp was right out in the country, at a place called Settingly, with a wood on one side, and a farm about half a mile away on the other; you got milk and eggs and butter from the farm, and there were usually the darlingest baby calves and piglets, and chickens. The camping-ground was high and airy, and everything smelt lovely when you woke in a tent and looked out, and the reveille sounded so jolly coming from the Captain's tent, instead of a dull old dressing bell. Every tent-leader had to answer the reveille on her whistle, to let the Captain know that the Guides were awake. You took your lunch out into the woods and made Nature notes, and in the evening found how much each Patrol had seen that was new

and interesting. Oh no, no ordinary school
rules, just a few camp laws that Miss Ferrars
read out at the beginning, and not difficult
ones to keep, really, except the non-talking
at night.

Brenda asked questions about everything,
and tried to think that it wouldn't be very
long to next summer and her turn ; and then
Peggy Wantage got an abscess in her tooth,
the very day before the campers were off to
Settingly.

Matron took poor Peggy to the dentist, a
handkerchief held to her very swollen face—
it appeared that she had been suppressing
toothache for two days for fear of losing the
camp—and was paying a price for it—and
Miss Christopherson sent for Brenda.

" My dear, would you like to go to camp
in poor Peggy's place ? "

" Oh, I would ! " Brenda cried ecstatically ;
" that is, if she really can't go."

" No, I certainly could not allow her to go
to camp to-morrow with so bad an abscess ;
at the best she cannot be fit before Sunday,
and then it is possible Miss Ferrars could
squeeze her in for the last day, if I am able
to send her over. But you are quite entitled
to her place, my dear, if you care to take it,
and I should be very glad for you to have

the opportunity. The others in your Patrol
are junior to you, Katharine assures me, so
yours would be the next chance."

"You don't know how I've been longing to
camp," Brenda confessed, and Miss Christopherson smiled kindly.

"I hope you will enjoy it very much
indeed. I think I should like to tell you that
your friend Mariota came to Miss Ferrars
and offered you her place, because you had
never camped ; but it was agreed between
Miss Ferrars and myself that it would not do
to change the rules in your case. But I am
particularly glad that your chance has come
in this way. . . . About your equipment,
Peggy will, I am sure, lend you her linen hat,
which is, I understand, wanted in camp, and
I have no doubt that Mariota will see to
your having everything else that is wanted
in the way of blankets, tin plates, etc. Go
and consult with her. . . ."

"And say thank you ; it *was* nice of her
to think of giving me her place," said
Brenda, and withdrew rapidly, hardly able
to believe her luck.

.   .   .   .   .   .

Brenda felt that she was really living in a
story of adventure, when the great lorries
rolled up at Beech House at eight o'clock

punctually next morning, and the work of packing in began, with a good deal of noise and of fun. Untidy, knobby bundles of kit were thrust in for seats, and a huge hamper containing to-day's lunch ready cooked, for the experienced Miss Ferrars declared it would be all they could do to get the tents pitched, and the wash-house screening up before dinner, and that camp cookery must wait till supper-time.

" Shall I cook ? " asked Brenda.

" Can you ? " Margaret wished to know.

" I can make toffee," Brenda said, and every one in hearing laughed.

" We'll teach you to make a lot more things than that," Margaret said kindly. " Everybody takes a turn at doing everything in camp, you know ; so you get to learn a lot."

The packing of the lorries took a good half-hour, but the last lot of kit was pushed in at last, and the navy-clad crowd had found seats, and hats were waved to Miss Christopherson, who stood at the door, smiling serenely at the noise, and the lorries got under way and were off, with Miss Ferrars in one and Miss Kean in the other, and twenty excited Guides in charge of each.

They sang all the way as soon as they had

left the streets behind them, and Miss Ferrars made no objection.   Shades of Nystrea ! Brenda, shouting choruses with the rest, thought of her stiff walks and drives, with a governess talking on instructive subjects, or telling her not to stoop, or to stride, or to put hands in her coat-pockets.   All that seemed a long way off to-day.

The great clumsy lorries took nearly an hour and a half to cover the twelve miles, but nobody minded either the slowness or the shaking, though there was a vigorous cheer from the foremost lorry-load when the farm came in sight, and they knew that they were practically there.   A huge, awkward lad, with a rather vacant but kindly face, shuffled forward with a grin to hold open a wide field gate.

" Hold tight, Guides ! " shouted Miss Ferrars, as the lorries lurched and jolted through the gate and slowly up the long field.

The foremost drew up opposite a wide gap in a hawthorn hedge, and the Beech House Guides saw before them the slope and low scrub of the camping-ground and the army hut for emergency, and the rolls of tents and poles which had been sent from London to be there before them.

" Now, Guides, down and stack the kit

till we're ready for it," Miss Ferrars cried;
" then sit in a circle, and Margaret will give
out a bun and a drink of lemonade to everybody, before we start setting up our camp."

Brenda, sitting between M. M. and
Katharine, eating her bun, and taking a
drink from one of the six tin mugs which
Margaret had condescended to unpack at
this stage, thought life was being gloriously
worth while at last !

CHAPTER XVIII

A NIGHT ALARM

EVERYBODY worked at top speed, and if a few mistakes were made, they were put right in all good humour. Brenda discovered that hammering in tent-pegs that will keep guy ropes as firm as they require to be, is not done perfectly by the light of Nature, and requires a little practice; fixing the high walls of sacking-screening round the specially prepared poles sent with it, to form the six little separate cubicles for washing, was extraordinarily difficult at first. Grease-pits, etc., had been dug before-hand by one of the farm labourers, but there was plenty left for the girls to do, and they were one and all thoroughly hot and tired by the time the Captain's whistle sounded the P.L.'s call to " Run in."

Brenda, who had been put on to collecting firewood, after her fifth tent-peg had come up at the first pull on it, was near enough to hear what was said.

" Robins, unpack the plates, knives and

forks, mugs and spoons. Swallows, get the
long strip of white mackintosh, and spread
it in the shade for a tablecloth, then lay the
table, and go to Miss Kean for the provisions.
Wrens, take buckets to the stream, and fill
up the big kettle ; there will be washing-up
to do after dinner, and we must have some
water hot. Put one bucket ready for people
to wash their hands in before dinner.
Canaries, get the fire alight ; the water must
go on before lunch—it takes ages to boil.
Thrushes——"

What the members of the Thrush Patrol
were to do Brenda did not hear, for Katharine
was already hunting up her Swallows to get
on to this fresh job at the double. Brenda
wasn't altogether sorry to leave the firewood job, which is rather back-breaking in
the midday sun of a particularly hot July
day.

The four Swallows flew for Miss Kean, who
was busily unpacking and sorting at the
entrance to the stores tent, one of the very
first to go up. Katharine took possession
of a great roll of white mackintosh, its
advantage being that it could and did gather
up crumbs at the end of each meal instead of
leaving them on the grass, and could be
washed down after being used. Brenda set

out twenty enamel plates, with a knife,
fork, and spoon to each, upon either side of
the long strip, and one at each end for
Captain and Lieutenant. M. M. followed
her closely with a great bag containing meat
patties, two for each Guide : she had to go
back to Miss Kean for a second bagful. A
large currant bun was further put by the
plate of every girl, and two apples. The
enamel mugs were filled with raspberry
vinegar and water. Katharine went the
round, pouring from a big enamel jug, and
Miss Ferrars whistled the " Guides come
up ! Guides come up ! Guides come up !
Do ! " the threefold repetition of the three
short notes, and then the one long, for the
" *Do* " — which brought the Company
doubling up, hot and thirsty and hungry,
too, despite the thirst, from their various
occupations. Grace was said, and lunch
attacked with vigour. The Swallows took
it in turns to fetch fresh supplies of drink
from the stores tent for the thirsty
crowd, and Brenda took her turn with the
rest.

When every one had finished, Miss Ferrars
gave out notices.

" The Swallows clear and wash up now ;
the washing will be an easy business,

Swallows, nothing greasy. You ought to be through in a quarter of an hour, if you're quick. Then everybody is to take their rugs to some shady spot and rest silently for an hour. It wouldn't hurt you to go to sleep; and I dare say you'll find it's quite easy. After the silence hour, Guides may talk, but are not to get up till I blow my whistle, which will be at 3.30. Blackbirds and Thrushes, you are responsible for tea, which will be at 4.30. There is the menu, bread and jam, as much as any one can eat, and one slice of cake round. Use the strawberry jam to-day; go to Miss Kean for stores, get the kettle on early, and cover the bread and jam with the cloths I gave you, because of wasps and flies. Swallows, Wrens, and Canaries will report to me at the hut, where our straw for stuffing palliasses has been put. Bring the mattress covers with you; you saw where we piled them, Katharine. If we work hard we can have every mattress ready stuffed and in its right place by tea-time. Bantams, get the ground-sheets unpacked, and spread out in the tents, one to go under each palliasse.

"Margaret, you understand the making of camp washstands; the Robins are to fit up the washing cubicles. Chaffinches, here

is the tent list for you; collect the suit-cases
and labelled kit, and dump the right things
down by every tent. Woodpeckers, go to
the farm for the drinking water and milk;
the tea-patrols will want it by four—not a
minute later. Tits, you must divide yourselves between getting firewood and washing-up water; the big tank by the hut will
want filling up. I shan't tell you again;
everybody get on to their own stunts at the
double when my whistle goes after the rest-
time; now stand for grace ! ''

The Swallows didn't waste a minute in
getting on to their job, and cleared with
lightning speed. But the washing-up was
a longer business than Brenda at least had
expected; she had never done such a thing
in her life before. Two of the Robins came
to help good-naturedly, and there was plenty
of fun and laughter over the work.

Both Robins had camped last year, it
appeared from their talk.

" 'Member the Morse alphabet that
Margaret made up about us ? '' Pat Wyott
said.

" Yes; wasn't it a scream, and awfully
clever ! '' Katharine answered. " She had
three ' Nancies,' hadn't she ? and not a
single O., or S., or B., or Z., of course.''

" We've got a B. now, anyway," M. M. said,
grinning.   " Some B. too !

" B. is for Brenda, come of royal estate,
  But she takes ten minutes to wash one plate ! "

Everybody shouted, even Katharine, and
Brenda didn't find the easiest thing in the
world to keep her temper.   But she managed
not to show that she minded rather being
labelled as incompetent ; after all, M. M.
had been very decent in offering to give up
her place in camp.

" All right for B. ; now I'll give you another
letter—M.," she said.

" M., Mariota, who sometimes is right,
  But she never stops teasing from morning to night."

Several people thumped Brenda upon
the back in token of approval, Mariota
herself among the foremost. Brenda discovered that she was felt to have kept her
end up creditably ; but none the less did she
hope for an opportunity of doing something
to distinguish herself before the finish of
the camp. It might be wholesome, but it
wasn't pleasant to find herself inferior to
everybody else in all practical things.

The rest of the day passed at top speed.
Brenda went right off to sleep after her

strenuous morning, and didn't rouse till K. and M. M. had been talking plans over her for several minutes in voices which weren't lowered at all.

It appeared that four ribbons were given out at the close of each day, and your Patrol won these ribbons by the marks the Patrol's different members had gained. " White for neatness, blue for braininess—it counts for that if somebody thinks sensibly in a difficulty," M. M. explained; " red for good and punctual work on our stunts ; green for good Nature observation. We Swallows are going to stick up totem poles outside our tents, and every ribbon we get can be fixed on to it. There'll be inspection both of us and our tent every morning, Brenda; so mind you're tidy, and polish your belt. If we get some free time after tea, as we're sure to do, we'll make some gadgets for our tent ; only four in it means plenty of room, and it's awfully nice to have a shoe-rack for your spare shoes, and a rail or two for hanging clothes, and somewhere to put your sponge. We'll look out some decent sticks presently, and I've brought lots of string. We might get a mark or so towards the blue ribbon if we think of some really brainy gadgets."

" What about making camp-stools ? "

asked Brenda. " Of course the ground is
bone dry to-day, but it mightn't be always."

" Oh, we use ground sheets if it's wet or
doubtful, and in the tent we have the suit-
cases that have our change of clothes."

Brenda was again reminded of her own
inadequacy ; she might have thought of that.
Never mind, she would do *something* for the
winning of a ribbon later on. The Captain's
whistle shrilled out before she had time to
think what.

Tea was only three minutes late—" very
good for the first day," Miss Ferrars pro-
nounced. The palliasses were finished, too,
and all laid out on ground sheets in the tents
by tea-time. Brenda didn't distinguish herself particularly or the reverse ; there wasn't
much scope for it. Miss Ferrars took one
from each Patrol for the clearing and washing-up, and sent the rest to unpack and make
their beds and their tents ready. Judy
Kerne was the Swallow chosen, and Brenda
went joyfully with Katharine and M. M., and
then and there took her first lesson in " square
lashing," and helped Katharine in the making
of a shoe-rack for the tent.

They had all petitioned for a camp-fire ;
but Miss Ferrars refused. Every one would
be tired after the strenuous business of pre-

paring camp, and she wanted them in bed before dark ; it took so much longer then.

" But I won't blow the silence whistle for half an hour after you're in bed," she pro-mised ; " so you can talk and enjoy your-selves. You won't find you're sorry to lie down."

They weren't. The palliasses were quite unexpectedly comfortable, and it was de-lightful to stretch out luxuriously and talk, with the bell-tent opening looped back to let in the soft, sweet, cool air across the slope, with its low bushes, to the level space below the hut where they would hoist the Colours to-morrow morning ; and beyond, soft, velvety dark shading away into the deep blackness of the wood.

" Tell us a story, M. M., as we were done out of the camp-fire," demanded Judy. " She tells topping stories," was added for Brenda's benefit.

So M. M. told a highly thrilling one about a Guide camp, which had chosen its site just over the hidden den of a gang of anarchists, who when in danger of detection played the ghost in a white sheet, and were only thwarted, just as they were planning to assassinate the King and Queen on their way to open an Agricultural Show,

by the intrepidity and daring of a Guide,
who deduced with the skill of a Sherlock
Holmes, signalled the police, and, pending
their arrival, blew an S.O.S. call on the
Captain's whistle, which roused the camp,
who rushed out armed with pepper for the
blinding of the foe.

The story had reached this exciting point
when a whistle thrilled out, not the S.O.S.
call, but the Captain's Silence Order.

" We must shut shop, M. M.; thanks
awfully for the topping yarn. Comfortable,
everybody ? Good-night," Katharine said.

She turned over, and there was a virtuous
silence in the tent.

Brenda couldn't go to sleep. She had
been a good deal sleepier before M. M.'s story
than she was now. She couldn't get it out
of her mind, and the sounds of the outdoor
night-world seemed extraordinarily loud now
she was awake in a sleeping camp. She
came untucked and was cold. She dozed a
little and woke again, and dozed again, all
without losing the sense of cold and consciousness of the sounds of the night-world.

She had been doing this for a long time
when she remembered that Katharine had
told her to spread her mackintosh over her
bed if she should feel at all cold in the night.

For some minutes after she remembered that she tried to think that she wasn't really cold, because it required such an effort to unroll from her palliasse and stumble across the tent in the dark.

But she was cold, and you can't go to sleep when you are really cold ; at last she got up, felt for her gym shoes, put them on, and stumbled towards the suit-case on which they had laid the pile of macks, which served as dressing-gowns in camp. She got hold of one, and with it hanging loosely round her shoulders, prepared to feel her way back to her own mattress. She had to pass the opening of the tent, and stood still for a moment to look out. The world was velvet dark—there wasn't even a star. All that soft blackness, except for . . .

Brenda gave a great jump, and M. M.'s story flew into her mind ; it had never been very far distant from it. For something dimly white was moving towards her, something that paused at intervals, as though in search of some hidden opening beside a bush, exactly as the horrible deformed anarchist of M. M.'s story had done.

It was these pauses that decided Brenda ; the " thick-set, grey-white shape," to quote M. M., had kept his hiding-place under a great bush of gorse, and two seconds after he had entered it no one could have told where he had disappeared.

Shivering all over, but determined to show herself a real Guide, Brenda made a dash for Katharine's suit-case; her belt would be on the top of her pile of clothes with the whistle attached, because she would have to answer the réveillé call for her tent. Brenda fell over the shoe-rack, and sent shoes flying, but she found the belt and whistle, and, putting all her strength into the effort, sent the S.O.S. call out into the sleeping camp as loudly as she could. Three short, three long, three short; and then again and yet again.

Somebody grasped and pulled away the whistle. " *Brenda!* " was all the horrified Katharine had time to cry, before the Captain's electric torch was flashing among them, and the Captain's voice was demanding angrily:

" Who is making that idiotic noise? "

Brenda had certainly fulfilled her intention of waking the camp; everywhere the pale glancing lights of electric torches; Miss Kean was hurrying up asking anxiously if some one was ill. Patrol Leaders were at the doors of their tents; everywhere was a buzz of sleepy questioning.

Poor Brenda endeavoured to explain, but she didn't get far.

" An anarchist! A ghost! What are you talking about ? " Miss Ferrars said. " There's nothing here "—she flashed her torch round—" except the farmer's old white pony, which sometimes wanders up through the gap from the field. How could you be so silly ? "

Poor Brenda was speechless, but M. M., though choking with laughter, came valiantly to the rescue.

" It was all my fault ; I told a story about anarchists got up as ghosts, and hiding under a camp . . ."

" Go back to bed, every one, and do try and tell something more sensible next time," the Captain said, but less angrily. " And another night, Brenda, if you really think something is wrong, put on your shoes and mack and come to me. *Never* blow a whistle and wake every one. Now, I'll tuck you up ; you're as cold as ice, and here is a biscuit for you. Go to sleep, and let every one else do the same."

" I'm very sorry," poor Brenda murmured—and almost thought she would have a cold next morning, and ask to go home.

But she didn't ; for all that the camp

considered her " anarchist " the joke of the season, and ragged her considerably. It was good-natured ragging, though, and Brenda acknowledged on reflection that she had been idiotic. She had been half asleep and obsessed by M. M.'s story : that was her only excuse, and it wasn't a very good one; still, some how by the end of next day she was finding it quite possible to laugh at herself, and at the verse with which M. M. commemorated her exploit, and which was to be written in the Log-Book, profusely illustrated, with photographs, to which the Beech House Guides added after every camp :

" B. stands for Brenda, great on S.O.S.
Pony, ghost, or anarchist ?—which she could not guess.
W. for whistle, and W—hat the Captain said !
G. for Guides all giggling, and hustled back to bed ! "

CHAPTER XIX

THE EVE OF THE RALLY

THE end of term was very near. Girls were making plans for meeting in the holidays and for walking together, or sharing rooms next term.

" You'll stay with us, won't you, Brenda ? " asked M. M., and Brenda said, " Rather ! " with enthusiasm. It was nice to think that K. and M. M. really wanted her company, for their seniority would have entitled them to one of the coveted two-bed rooms next term, if they put in for it.

People were beginning to mark off days ; notices were going up on the board about returning library books, about applying for journey - money. The last Saturday had come, with its company meeting judged by two district commissioners for the Shield—a company meeting when every Guide, though a shade jumpy inwardly, played up to the top notch.

Roll-call absolutely slick ; message to be memorised signalled to the whole company by Miss Kean; original Nature game explained clearly, though in the high-pitched voice of inward nervousness, by Margaret Reresby, and played with gusto; memorised message written down by every Guide and handed in to Captain, squad of twenty drilled on the hard court by Miss Kean; twenty working round the table in Junior Common Room at Toymaker's Badge (the results of which were already booked for the Children's Ward in the local hospital), under the guidance of the Blackbird P.L., who had passed in the badge brilliantly last year. The Captain with another squad in School Hall working for the Child Nurse Badge, the smallest Brownie as model. And then illustrated badges, one to each Patrol; leaders drawing for them, and the Swallows getting fire-brigade, which they had just passed in bulk, and enjoying themselves to the extent of forgetting that they were being inspected for general efficiency and a Shield; and the Commissioners expressing themselves pleased, though guardedly, and Miss Ferrars of the opinion that all had gone very creditably.

On Monday the competitors from each Guide Company of Rotherbay would swim for the Cup, with judges watching from a boat, and on Tuesday was the Rally at the recreation ground : exhibitions of drill, and signalling, and a model camp in one corner ; then the presentation of the Cup and the Shield to the winning Companies, the march past, the saluting base, tea in the grounds for all and sundry, Guides and spectators, and after tea, the Pageant.

Wednesday packing, and Thursday going home.

Count and Countess Wrynder were coming to the Rally, with their children, and the Countess had written to Brenda that, with Miss Christopherson's permission, they would drive the Princess and the Crown Prince up to town with them on Wednesday evening, as it would be more convenient for the escort provided for their journey.

" I wonder why the Countess doesn't say who is coming," Brenda said to M. M. " I hope it's Miss Heron : I should like you to see her."

But really there was too much else to think about just then to worry over escorts.

The term had simply raced, Brenda thought, since the Guide camp, which had been so jolly and successful that she had long ago forgotten to feel sore about her ridiculous blunder of the first night. The last Sunday had passed by, and here was the eve of the Rally, and at three o'clock she was swimming in the team race for the Cup. .

Eighteen out of the thirty Guide Companies of Rotherbay were competing, and you had to be first in diving, single, and team race all together to win the Swimming Cup. Brenda was one of the two Guides for the team race.

" Now keep steady," Margaret urged, as she walked down with the swimming competitors. " You team-race people are apt to rush it at first, and it's rather a long course, remember. And I hear the Node College girls are bigger than you are, and hot stuff ; that means an advantage in stroke."

" We'll be as cool as ice-cream," M. M., who partnered Brenda in the two team, promised fervently.

The single race came first ; Peggy Royce, the Wren P.L., was the Company champion.

" You'll be it next year," M. M. told Brenda with confidence, as they selected their spot for watching the race. " You were in the running for this, but Margaret said you were too young. But your style is just topping ; they mark for style, you know, as well as for speed."

" M. M., did Margaret really say so ? Why,

she was so down on me at the beginning for wanting to swim for the Cup ? "

" You thought too much of yourself," M. M. stated, with candour. " You've got a bit more sense now, and Margaret told Glenna Graham that you were ' a topping kid ' ; I heard her."

" She generally tells me not to be so abysmally stupid about something or another," Brenda laughed.

" Margaret would ; don't you worry. I say, she's sure to go top in the diving, isn't she ? "

" Couldn't help it," Brenda was certain.

" I wish the diving came first ; I'd rather see Margaret dive than Peggy swim."

" So would I ; there won't be time, I suppose ? "

" No ; Miss Ferrars said we were to get into our bathing things as soon as the first race was over ; they don't take long over the diving. But Katharine has promised to come and tell us the very second she knows ; some luck for us she's a ' delicate ' and not swimming, though rough on her."

It was dead high water, and the competitions would take place quite close inshore for the benefit of the spectators.

The judges were in boats, and a couple of

the Rollincourt masters were feathering lazily, ready to hold the tape between their two boats, when the moment came. Brenda recognised Carol's friend, the young master who had been so cavalier in his treatment of her; three or four small boys were scrambling about in his boat, Carol among them.

"Hullo! there's Mr. Reresby—glad he's going to do one end of the tape," M. M. said cheerfully. "He's such a good sort."

Brenda thought she could have done without Mr. Reresby's presence very well, but she didn't say so, as M. M. seemed pleased.

"He's coming to the Rally too, and the Pageant," M. M. chattered on, "Margaret told me."

"Margaret! Does she like him too?" Brenda asked, rather disconcerted.

"I s'pose so; she's his sister," M. M. told her carelessly. "Hullo! there go the competitors, down that lane kept between the people. I bet Peggy's got the jim-jams by now, poor old thing. But she's sure to swim splendidly."

Eighteen competitors, shivering with nervousness, not cold, for the afternoon was really hot, stood at the water's brink, waiting the signal to wade or swim to their place

along the starting-tape, which was now being
stretched.   Mr. Reresby at the far end of
the course, where Brenda and M. M. had
fixed their stance upon a convenient break-
water, could be heard addressing the boys
with the same unvarnished plainness which
had so affronted Brenda when applied to
herself.

" Now then, you young ruffians, bunch up
into the bows out of my way, and don't
move an eyelid till they've finished this race.
I take the shore end, don't I, Hanson ?
Here's your end of the tape."

He rowed inshore, keeping in line with
the master in the other boat, till the judges
called " Halt ! " and the tape was stretched.

A District Commissioner stood ready, with
her whistle to her lips, to give the starting
signal.   The first stroke of three boomed
from the clock tower on the Parade, and
immediately after shrilled the starting
whistle.   The starting-tape was switched
away from under eighteen pairs of hands,
and the Guides were off.

" Peggy's fifth from the shore end, in the
pink-and-grey cap," M. M. said.   " I made
K. lend it her because it's so easy to spot."

The course was a hundred and fifty
yards ; for the first fifty the pink-and-grey

cap was not even in the first five, who had begun to pull away from the others almost at once.

" She did better than that in the tests," murmured Brenda uneasily.

Eighty yards saw a difference. The very tall girl with the yellow cap, who swam for Node College, had pulled away more definitely from the rest; she was nearly two lengths ahead. The blue cap which had been swimming next to her was dropping back a little; but the pink-and-grey was now in a line with the other four. "She's forging along!" M. M. whispered.

A hundred yards. Node House still two lengths ahead of anybody, but a black cap, who had been behind at the start, was making wonderful pace, and almost up with a green and a pink-and-grey, who were swimming neck to neck. A hundred and twenty. Black cap had passed green cap and pink-and-grey; yellow cap was splashing more in the effort to increase her pace. The other two kept steadily two lengths behind.

Spectators were getting excited; there was a general pressing forward and crowding up, and some one raised the cry of " Node College! Node!"

" Beech House!" yelled M. M., and several

people took that up, " Beech House ! Beech House ! "

For pink-and-grey was spurting, not too violently, but with judgment and decision. She was leaving blue cap and the rest behind, only in front of her black cap trod hard upon the heels of yellow.

" Cedars ! Node ! " shouted the crowd confusedly. " *Beech House !* "

Brenda and M. M. were past shouting now, for at a hundred and forty yards, pink-and-grey had passed black cap ! Yellow was still ahead and the tape was very near.

Little by little the distance between the two caps lessened—they were abreast. A wild cheer went up from everybody, as they clutched the tape absolutely together, Beech House and Node College—a tie !

.   .   .   .   .   .

A quarter of an hour later, and Brenda and M. M. stood looking at each other speechlessly. Upon the team - race competitors hung the winning or the losing of the Cup. For the first time since the Guide swimming competition had been started, there had been a tie for two events between the same two Companies. Margaret Reresby of Beech House and Sheila Fane of Node had both won absolutely full marks for their diving.

Not even M. M. found anything to say when Katharine brought them the news breathlessly.

"Ready, Guides, for the Two Team-Race?" That was Miss Ferrars at their cabin door, and the two came out, still speechless. Then Brenda said, "Oh, Miss Ferrars!" rather helplessly.

"Feeling like that?" laughed the Captain, though it is probable that she felt no more like laughing than the girls themselves did. "Don't worry; just swim your best, and we'll be proud of the second place."

Mariota was the starter, and took her place at the far end; Brenda opposite, behind the starting-tape, unable to move until M. M. touched her hand. The time seemed endless before the District Commissioner raised her whistle to her lips; and the distance, as she looked along towards the master's boats, with the tape between, seemed endless too. And the Node House girl who stood next to her, seemed absolutely enormous; Brenda thought forlornly that Node House seemed inhabited by a race of giants.

The whistle at last; and the starting competitors swimming like mad towards their partners in the race.

Brenda kept her eyes steadily on M. M.; she wasn't among the first, but, like Peggy, she seemed making way. That girl with the tremendous reach, who was passing her on the left, must be another of the Node House giants. (Brenda learned afterwards that there were three Mackenzie sisters swimming, and the shortest was 5 feet 11 inches.) She saw that girl because she had to see, but she had a feeling that if she took her eyes off M. M. for a moment she would lose the Beech House chance.

Nearer! Nearer! three in line and one ahead. The one ahead that huge Node House, of course. The Node House partner put out her hand; she would get the start of every one. Brenda put out hers from behind the tape, though it was much too soon.

" Steady, girls," shouted the judging Commissioner at this end. " Any Guide starting a second before she is touched disqualifies herself."

M. M. was spurting—every one was spurting—about seven seemed abreast, and then Node House touched her partner, and she was under the tape and off for the goal. M. M. and five others bore down upon the tape almost simultaneously only a quarter

of a minute later, M. M. just third; and
Brenda, too, was off — at last to fulfil
her term's ambition of swimming for the
school.

She mustn't use up all her strength
and breath at the start, though it was
maddening to see four people ahead of her
to begin with, and Node House very much
ahead.

Two people had passed her from behind by
half-way at the course, and Node House
was at least four lengths ahead. But
Brenda had been thoroughly at home in the
water for years, and she wasn't in the least
distressed up to date. She thought the
minute had come when she might risk
letting go — if Beech House were to hold
the Cup, she mustn't only forge ahead of
the Node House competitor, but sufficiently
far ahead to allow for the difference in
stretch; the first to grasp the tape was the
winner.

Brenda drew in one deep breath, then
went arm over arm for her life. She was
leaving the rest—the distance between herself and Node House was lessening steadily—
the cheering was one continuous ear-splitting
roar. She could hardly see—she was half-
choked with water, but the tape was just

ahead, gleaming taut above the green, and she had passed Node House.

Churning water—one wild clutch, and a swallow of sea-water with it. She had the tape, half a second first.

"*Beech House! Ourselves!*"

CHAPTER XX

BRENDA FINDS HER FEET

IT was the afternoon of the great Guide Rally. Thirty Companies from Rotherbay and its district were formed up in one great hollow square in the centre of the recreation ground.

Sitting in temporary grand stands, put up for the occasion, and standing on benches, or tiptoeing behind the Guides, a deeply interested crowd was seeing all it could.

The Divisional Commissioner, in bravery of silver cords and cockade, stood forward.

" I have much pleasure in announcing that the closely contested competition for the Guide Shield has been won this year by the IX Rotherbay Company, Beech House ! Three cheers for the winning Company ! "

The cheers thundered, as Miss Ferrars, radiant, marched up to receive the Shield. Brenda had never known before how Guides could cheer. She was so thrilled in listening that she was taken by surprise when some-

body gripped her arm, and turning, she saw
Margaret.

" Brenda, they're going to present the
Cup, and I want you to go up and take it."

" But—*I* didn't win it—at least only
partly," Brenda protested, forgetful, it is
to be feared, that she had received the
equivalent of an order from her Company
Leader. " You did the dive, and Peggy ! "

" We've settled you're to go ; we think
you deserve it," Margaret said ; and Brenda,
hardly able to believe her ears, gave in, only
saying firmly, " M. M. *must* come too, then ;
we were both in the Team."

" All right, both then," Margaret agreed,
and the two marched up together a moment
later to receive, with the congratulations of
the Commissioner, the Swimming Cup, and
the cheers of the whole vast crowd.

.   .   .   .   .   .

Tea was provided for the actors right
away from the grand stands, and the acting-
ground, close by the old, long-disused quarry,
which was to serve as their dressing-room.

So much low scrubs, gorse and black-
berry bushes clothed its brink that it was
possible for the actors to gain the trees
that fringed the back of the recreation ground
unperceived, and from their shelter make

their entrances on to the so-called "Village Green." The stream and the bridge were on the opposite side.

Brenda would have liked to find Carol, and hear what he thought of the March Past and the Rally generally ; but there was no time to spare for actors. Their tea was snatched anyhow in the intervals of hurrying out of Guide uniform and into their Pageant clothes, and the actors in the first episode were barely ready when a Guider had spoken the Prologue, so clearly and slowly that most of the audience heard what she said, and those who did not felt they should have.

Every Captain was in charge of her own Company episode, and discouraged talking lest it should disturb the Pageant.

But Miss Ferrars voyaged out when the time for " A Royalist Maid " was at hand, to make sure that the horses " off " the stage were ready at exactly the place where " Mistress Diana " and the King would look for them; and the actors in the episode just finished, who had camped the week-end after Beech House, had something to say to them, and said it.

" I say, who *do* you think is standing on the fence beyond the stream ? "

" Who ? " asked M. M., not that she cared

to know much, for " Peter " had to make
the first speech in the Royalist episode, and
she was feeling decidedly jumpy.

" That big boy at the camp farm who's
silly—you know, the one who opens gates.
They're all there, the farmer and his wife ;
they told me they were coming, and the
daughter, and they've brought the boy, and
he's loving it, only he will stand up on the
fence, all the time."

" I say, don't make such a row," said
Margaret, descending on them, looking very
handsome in the green livery suit and the
King's black wig, but also a little on edge.

The conversationalist moved away.

" The horses are all ready by the tree, as
at last rehearsal," Miss Ferrars said, returning ; " but Hughes is so sorry he has had
to change your mount, Margaret. It has
a damaged fetlock, but he declares he has
brought you a very quiet and well-behaved
steed. Oh, and I have asked Mr. Reresby
and Mr. Hanson to stand up this end of the
wood and help with the shouting behind the
scenes. It sounded a little thin. Beginners,
please ! "

" Good luck ! " whispered Brenda to
M. M., and then went and stood by her
" father," Glenna Graham, magnificent in

high boots, feathered hat, and a grey pointed beard.

The children danced on the green and were harshly stopped by the Roundhead soldiers. Peter overheard their talk, and expressed his intention of informing Mistress Diana of the intended close search for the King.

Diana had her scene with her timorous and time-serving father, and all led up excellently well to the spirited saving of the fugitive Charles II.

Margaret unbent to a surprising degree as the two stood together in the wood beside their horses, ready to mount at the speech before their entrance-cue.

" The audience are eating it, simply," she remarked. " Did you see our farm-people, and the boy ? They're thrilled. You really are doing your part awfully well, Brenda."

" Do you really think so ? " Brenda said. " It's ever so good of you to say that, Margaret. We shall both live this scene, anyway, and I hope the audience will. I love the bolt over the bridge—it's so real."

" Yes—s," Margaret agreed, but a shade doubtfully. " Time we mounted, isn't it ? I'd like a minute to settle to my steed, as I'm not used to it."

" He's all right, Miss Reresby," said the

riding-master, as he put her up. "A *leetle* hard about the mouth, that's all. Don't let him have his head."

"All right," Margaret said shortly, but Brenda had a fancy that she wasn't absolutely at ease upon the hard-mouthed horse. Should she offer to change mounts? It would sound as though she thought herself a much better rider than Margaret, though, and only yesterday M. M. had told her that she had thought too much of herself when she came; it would never do to let anybody, Margaret in especial, think she was swanky still. Besides, Margaret rode very well, only a little stiffly.

Miss Ferrars handed Margaret the pie; the cue was spoken by the Corporal-in-Command at the bridge, and Brenda and Margaret walked their horses out of the wood, and across the "green," Brenda leading. She was supposed to glance to right and left and all about to show the audience that Mistress Diana was seeking a way of escape for the fugitive behind her, and therefore was able half-unconsciously—for most people were a blur—to see the friendly farmer of Settingly and his family. Yes, as Margaret had said, they were thoroughly enjoying the Pageant; three of them sitting close under the fence on the other side of the stream, where they could certainly command a very good view of the scene at the bridge, and the fourth standing upon the fence, as though to see more, eyes and mouth both open.

" I'm glad they brought poor Jimmy," Brenda thought, for all the camp-girls had found Jimmy the most good-natured of boys in the way of emptying big buckets, or carrying any heavy load over the field for them, as they went to and fro from the farm. It had never seemed to matter that he wasn't quite as clever as some people. Then she had to concentrate upon the business of the play.

The scene at the bridge seemed likely to bring down the house, metaphorically speaking. Margaret had never acted better ; M. M. as Peter was really very funny, and Brenda lived in her part and loved it. There was not a hitch anywhere, and the fugitives were making their dash for freedom amid a tense silence of very real excitement from the thronged spectators.

Margaret, leading, was almost at the bridge when poor Jimmy's wild excitement got the better of him. He waved both his great arms like the sails of a windmill and broke into one of the harsh, discordant cries with which he was accustomed to express his pleasure.

Margaret's horse reared wildly, very nearly throwing her ; before she could recover her balance or her grip upon the reins, it had turned clean round and was galloping madly across the " green " to the other side of the recreation ground.

Brenda, occupied with her own dancing horse, hardly realised Margaret's plight as she flew past ; but was on to it, in a minute, and remembered what the riding-master had said about the hard mouth. The horse was bolting, and bolting badly, and nothing but very steady pulling on the reins could stop it, and that Margaret was not giving. The reins seemed to be hanging loose.

Brenda dashed in pursuit, her horse quite ready to second her desire to get as far away as possible from the ghastly noise and mysterious waving something on the fence, which had upset its nerves.

Brenda was half-way across the " green " when she thought of the quarry, straight for which the runaway was making. Hitherto she had only thought of stopping the bolting horse ; now she knew that somehow she must stop it in time, for there was no one else to do it.

No one ? Yes, some one, a man, in the rather shabby grey flannels that Mr. Reresby had been wearing, was tearing from the wood, evidently in the desperate attempt to get to the quarry first.

He couldn't do it possibly at the pace the bolting horse went, that was certain. Brenda redoubled her efforts, as she had done yesterday in the team-race, only now the stake was something infinitely more important than the winning of a cup.

She was not twenty yards from the brink of the quarry when she got abreast of the bolting horse and grabbed at Margaret's reins ; and she knew enough about horses to know quite well that there wouldn't be much to spare. It wants more strength than she possessed to stop a bolting horse, without a long and a steady pull. Mr. Reresby was straining every nerve to cross them before they came to the quarry, but he was on foot.

She got the loose reins, and gathered them into her right hand with an effort : now for the tug-of-war ! She must pull hard enough to check at least the flying pace of both the horses—at present both thundering down as hard as they could go upon the quarry.

Hundreds of people seemed running and

shouting, but no one was near enough to have
the remotest chance of doing anything, except
for Mr. Reresby, and he hadn't much—none,
if she couldn't check that frantic race. She
leaned back and pulled with all her might.

Margaret saw what she was at ; she was
gripping to the saddle with one hand, but she
got the other on the reins behind Brenda's
fist.

" Let go ! you'll be over," she gasped.

Brenda was suddenly horribly frightened,
frightened with a dryness of the mouth, and
a sinking feeling about her interior. For the
bushes fringing the mouth of the quarry
seemed jumping at her, and Mr. Reresby was
still yards away, and she did not think that
the pace had slackened for all her steady
pulling. But she set her teeth and pulled
on—and suddenly it *was* slower. Her arms
seemed wrenched out of their sockets ; but
Mr. Reresby had grasped at the reins of both
horses within rather less than a foot of the
quarry's brink.

Nobody spoke for a minute, only Margaret
put her hand over Brenda's ; then Brenda
remembered something, and held out her
hand to Mr. Reresby.

" We have met before," she said, " but I
am very glad to meet you again more

pleasantly. Thank you so much for coming to our rescue. I think you saved our lives."

Mr. Reresby seemed a little embarrassed as well as breathless.

" Much I could have done, if you hadn't half stopped 'em already," he said awkwardly, as he helped both the girls to dismount ; and then Brenda realised one reason why he felt shy. Several people were hurrying across the Pageant - ground towards them, and among the foremost she recognised Carol and—her father.

Brenda ran, heedless of the fact that her knees felt decidedly shaky, for King Conrad had actually taken enough interest in her concerns to come to Rotherbay to see the Rally.

" Father ! it's *so* nice to see you ! " she cried, with a warmth of welcome which she certainly had never bestowed on her father in her life before !

.   .   .   .   .   .

They finished the Pageant ; not the Royalist episode, which was considered to have finished itself. As Carol remarked cheerfully, when Brenda was planted on the grand stand between his father and himself, to watch the last two episodes : " You and your King Charles did a topping bolt, as far as that went."

" It's ' toppingness ' went rather far for me," remarked her father, and he actually drew Brenda's arm through his.

She was allowed to bring him back in triumph to Beech House, where he was more agreeable and less alarming than Brenda had ever known him to be. He thanked Miss Christopherson warmly for all that she had done for his daughter, and, on her whispered entreaty, requested permission to have the pleasure of her company and that of Brenda and three of her friends to dine at his hotel that evening. Brenda thereupon presented Katharine, Mariota, and, after a moment's trepidation, Margaret, explaining to her parent carefully that Margaret was Captain of B. House. She hoped he grasped the distinction ; in any case he was very gracious to them all, and told Margaret that he was also to have the pleasure of entertaining her resourceful brother to-night ; he and a couple of boys were Carol's guests this evening.

M. M. nudged Margaret and whispered : Margaret looked doubtful. M. M. uplifted her voice :

" Please—sir—if you weren't here, the

whole school would be giving Brenda three cheers, because of the Cup and her sportingness with the horses.   Margaret is afraid it isn't etiquette when you're here, but Miss Christopherson says you're taking Brenda back with you to town to-morrow morning, so it's the last chance."

" Mariota ! " said Miss Christopherson, rather shocked, but King Conrad smiled.

" Pray don't allow me to interfere with any customs of the school, Miss Mariota."

" Thank you very much, sir," Margaret said most properly, and then she shed her strict propriety and became the B. House Captain again.

" I know we all want to show Brenda what we think of her, so—three cheers for Brenda of Nystrea ! "

Nobody appeared to remember the conduct marks, or the quarantine, or the waking up the whole Guide camp ; Beech House nearly yelled the hall down. Brenda could hardly believe her ears ; all her efforts to do popular or distinguished things and make herself a person of importance had turned out so badly, and now the girls were cheering her for a thing that anybody would have done, and which she had hardly realised to be dangerous until the last minute. It wasn't exactly deserved, but it was rather pleasant, all the same.

"Thanks awfully, Margaret and everybody," she said, when they had finished. "But mightn't it be Brenda of Beech House as well as of Nystrea?—because I *am*!"

They gave her a deafening supplementary cheer as "Brenda of Beech House!"

THE END